Previously on Nanny Piggins . . .

Here we are at the sixth book. If this is the first Nanny Piggins book you've picked up you're probably wondering – What's going on? Who are these characters? Why did Great Aunt Gertrude buy me the sixth book in a series? (Just be grateful she got you this and not hand-knitted underwear.)

Anyway, let me assure you that it doesn't matter if you haven't read any of the previous books. They are all separate stories and you'll easily pick up who the characters are. If you don't believe me, here are a few handy pointers to get you started . . .

In the beginning, Nanny Piggins (The World's Greatest Flying Pig) came to live with the Green family after running away from the circus. Fortunately for the Green children – Derrick, Samantha and Michael – she was even better at nannying than she was at being blasted out of a cannon. Who could not love a nanny who thought attending school five days in a row was a danger to your health?

But their father, Mr Green, did not think so highly of Nanny Piggins, because he found it embarrassing that she was a pig (even worse, she was a startlingly attractive pig who terrified him).

Then Nanny Piggins' brother, Boris (a ten-foot-tall dancing bear) also ran away from the circus and came to live in the garden shed. Mr Green still has not noticed this. He is not an observant man.

There is also a lovely police sergeant, a highly acclaimed tap-dancing lawyer, a hygiene-obsessed rival nanny, identical fourteenuplet sisters, Hans the baker, Princess Annabelle (his royal wife), a retired army colonel and a whole swag of arch-nemeses.

I know it sounds confusing but trust me, you'll figure it out as you go along, because I always explain who people are as they appear (my publishers force me to). So just sit back, have a big bite of chocolate cake and start reading.

Best wishes,
R. A. Spratt, the author

Nanny Piggins

AND THE PURSUIT OF JUSTICE

BOOK 6

R. A. SPRATT

RANDOM HOUSE AUSTRALIA

To Diggy Doo

A Random House book
Published by Random House Australia Pty Ltd
Level 3, 100 Pacific Highway, North Sydney NSW 2060
www.randomhouse.com.au

First published by Random House Australia in 2012

Addresses for companies within the Random House Group can be found at
www.randomhouse.com.au/offices

National Library of Australia
Cataloguing-in-Publication Entry

Author: Spratt, R. A.
Title: Nanny Piggins and the Pursuit of Justice
ISBN: 978 1 86471 816 4
Series: Nanny Piggins; 6.
Target Audience: For primary school age
Dewey Number: A823.4

Cover illustration by Gypsy Taylor
Cover design by Christabella Designs
Internal design by Jobi Murphy
Internal illustrations by R. A. Spratt
Typeset in Adobe Garamond by Midland Typesetters, Australia
Printed in Australia by Griffin Press, an Accredited ISO AS/NZS 14001:2004
Environmental Management System printer.

Contents

CHAPTER 1

Nanny Piggins gets in Trouble

'You ought to be thoroughly ashamed of yourself!' yelled Nanny Piggins.

Nanny Piggins and the children were sitting outside the editor's office at their local newspaper. They were waiting for him to turn up so that Nanny Piggins could tell him off for the terrible suggestions given in his paper's advice column. And while they waited, Nanny Piggins was practising what she was going to say.

'I wouldn't use your newspaper to line the bottom of a budgerigar's cage!' hollered Nanny Piggins. (She enjoyed a good telling off once she got into full swing.) 'You aren't good enough to lie beneath budgie poop!'

'Don't you mean "your newspaper isn't good enough to lie beneath budgie poop"?' asked Derrick.

'I mean exactly what I say,' declared Nanny Piggins, before turning to Samantha. 'Did you get that all down?'

'I think so,' said Samantha, looking up from her notepad, 'but how do you spell budgerigar?'

'If you're not sure, just put "parrot",' suggested Nanny Piggins.

The rest of the newspaper staff were enjoying Nanny Piggins' visit tremendously. They were even chipping in with suggestions of mean things she could say. 'Tell him he's lazy,' suggested the editor's secretary.

'No, tell him everybody knows he wears a toupee,' suggested a girl cadet journalist.

'But he doesn't wear a toupee,' argued the senior copy editor. (She knew this because she'd had occasion to pull the editor's hair very hard during her last contract negotiation.)

'I know,' said the girl cadet journalist, 'which is why telling him we know he wears a toupee will really freak him out.'

'I won't have time to talk to the editor about his hair, no matter how bad it may be,' said Nanny Piggins. 'I will be too busy denouncing him for the terrible advice your paper gives big-boned readers.'

Boris wept loudly here, because he was one of those bigger-boned readers. (And that is not just a figure of speech. Being a ten-foot-tall dancing bear, his bones really were a lot larger.)

'Telling people to "stop eating cake"!' ranted Nanny Piggins. 'I've never heard such terrible advice! Everyone knows if you want to lose weight the best thing to do is exercise. And if you are going to take up exercise, obviously you need to eat *more* cake to give you the energy for all that running around.'

The staff in the open-plan office nodded at the wisdom of this. Nanny Piggins had brought a large caramel cream cake with her to provide tangible evidence for her argument. And the office staff had to agree that since having several large slices each they all felt considerably perkier.

'Now where was I?' asked Nanny Piggins.

Samantha read back over her notes. 'You had just finished telling him he had the intellectual capacity of a lump of lichen and had moved on to telling him he was unworthy of being covered in parrot droppings.'

'Ah yes,' said Nanny Piggins, regaining her train of thought. 'Had I told him I had a good mind to bite his shins yet?'

'Um . . . shins, no,' said Samantha, scanning the notes.

'Good,' said Nanny Piggins. 'I don't want to give him any forewarning.'

At this moment the hapless editor returned from lunch. As it turns out he was actually a big-boned man himself, so eating lunch was the high-light of his day. And Friday lunch was the highlight of his week, because that's when he would take an important advertiser with him to a fancy restaurant and charge the whole thing to the newspaper's credit card. So at three o'clock on Friday afternoon, after a four-course lunch with three extra side dishes, he was looking forward to getting back to the office, closing his door and having a nice long nap.

'That's him,' hissed the copy boy.

Nanny Piggins watched the editor as he lumbered along the central aisle of the open-plan area. 'Good gracious!' she exclaimed. 'His hair really is dreadful. I'm amazed any of you ever get any work done when you could spend all your time staring at it, or trying to poke it to see if it's a well-trained rodent sitting on his head.'

'Who's this?' asked the editor, mopping his brow. (The combination of eating an enormous lunch and then walking all the way from the lift had made him work up a sweat.)

'I am Sarah Matahari Lorelai Piggins,' announced Nanny Piggins, puffing up to her full four feet of height, 'and I have come here today to denounce you, sir! For –'

Nanny Piggins suddenly stopped talking.

'What's wrong?' asked Michael.

'Shhh,' said Nanny Piggins as she carefully sniffed the air.

'What's the meaning of this?' asked the editor. He was beginning to get upset because Nanny Piggins was blocking his path to the large comfy sofa in his office. 'I demand to know – mmpfff!'

The editor stopped talking here because Nanny Piggins had whipped a chocolate chip cookie out of her handbag and shoved it into his mouth to silence him.

'Be quiet,' she urged. 'I can smell something.'

Now everyone in the open-plan office was sniffing about.

'What is it?' whispered Derrick.

Nanny Piggins sniffed some more. A few short exploratory sniffs, then one long deep sniff, sucking in so much air around her that papers rustled and the editor's secretary had to grab the desktop photograph of her children to stop it being sucked into Nanny Piggins' nose.

'I smell cake,' whispered Nanny Piggins. All thoughts of the editor and revenge were now totally forgotten.

'Of course you do,' said Samantha. 'You brought in a lovely caramel cream cake when we arrived.'

'And it was delicious, thank you,' said the crime reporter.

'Yes, but it's gone now,' said Nanny Piggins. 'Now I smell another cake. It's got chocolate, cherries –' she sniffed some more – 'cream, sprinkles and –' She sniffed again – 'strawberry jam!'

'That sounds tasty,' said Boris. The prospect of cake had made him stop weeping for a moment.

'We must have some,' declared Nanny Piggins.

'But where is it?' asked Michael.

Nanny Piggins was sniffing side to side in a tracking pattern as she slowly made her way in the direction of the cake. She climbed over desks and journalists as she tracked down the delicious smell, until her snout was pressed hard against a sheet glass window.

'There it is!' exclaimed Nanny Piggins, pointing to the high-rise building opposite. 'Quick! Someone bring me something to smash the glass.'

'Couldn't you just open the window?' suggested Samantha.

'Oh yes,' said Nanny Piggins, 'I suppose that would work too.' She lifted the sash and leaned out into the fresh air, inhaling deeply. 'I was right! Chocolate cream cherry cake with a strawberry jam centre. And . . .' she inhaled deeply again, 'the words *Happy Birthday* written in solid chocolate on the top.'

'Come on,' said one of the more cynical journalists. 'How can she possibly sniff that?'

'Nanny Piggins,' Michael informed him seriously, 'can do anything.'

There was a crowd gathered around Nanny Piggins now as they stood looking out the window. In the building opposite they could see a lovely cake sitting on the table in the break room as a young woman put candles on the top.

'Candles! Definitely a birthday cake!' declared Nanny Piggins.

'You see,' said Michael proudly.

'There's no time to lose,' said Nanny Piggins. 'We must get over there or we'll miss out.'

'It's just a cake,' said the bloated editor.

Nanny Piggins grabbed him by the lapels and shook him. 'Get a grip of yourself, man,' she said. 'Do you know what you're saying?'

'Sorry,' said the editor.

'I need a rope and a grappling hook,' declared Nanny Piggins. 'Do any of you keep those things in your desks?'

The newspaper employees all shook their heads.

'No wonder you publish such a dreadful newspaper,' said Nanny Piggins, turning to the editor once more. 'You obviously haven't trained your staff properly if they aren't equipped to launch an assault on a neighbouring building without a moment's notice.'

'Sorry,' said the editor again.

'Never mind,' said Nanny Piggins. 'I'll just have to improvise. Derrick, fetch me the fire hose from that wall over there. Michael, fetch me the largest hole punch you can find. And Samantha, fetch me the plate the caramel cream cake was on so I can lick it clean. If I'm going to get to that chocolate cake I'll need all the energy I can muster.'

A few moments later Nanny Piggins had entirely

unravelled the fire hose, tied the hole punch to the end and was swinging it in large circles about her head as she leaned out the office window.

'Wouldn't it be easier just to go downstairs in our lift, walk across the road, then go upstairs in their lift to get to the cake,' suggested the editor.

'There's no time for that!' said Nanny Piggins. 'They'll start singing Happy Birthday soon, and once the candles are blown out, it's all over. I know what office workers are like. They're so bored out of their brains, they'll fall on that cake like a swarm of locusts. Anything to break the monotony.'

Nanny Piggins threw the hose-tethered hole punch and then watched as it sailed high through the air, smashed in through the window opposite and caught on the window frame.

'Aaaagggghhh,' screamed the young woman preparing the cake.

'You there!' Nanny Piggins called to her. 'Tie my hose to the door handle of your refrigerator. I'm coming over.'

The young woman did as she was told. Fortunately she had been a Girl Guide so she knew the knots for everything from rigging a sailing ship to detaining a terrorist with nothing but your shoelaces.

'What do you mean you're going over there?' panicked Samantha. 'This is a twelve-storey building.'

'Yes,' said Nanny Piggins, 'but it's only twenty metres from here to there. I'll just tightrope walk over and back. It'll take no time, and I'll bring you back a slice of cake.'

'But you can't tightrope walk across that,' protested Derrick.

'Why not?' asked Nanny Piggins.

'It's a hose,' said Derrick.

'I know,' agreed Nanny Piggins, 'and therefore it is wider than the tightropes we used at the circus. But hopefully the tightrope purists won't hold it against me when I explain that it is for a good cause – eating cake.'

'But it's not like tightrope walking inside the Big Top,' said Michael. 'This is outside. And it's a windy day.'

'Don't worry,' said Nanny Piggins. 'I don't mind if my hair gets a little windswept.'

'But what if you fall?' wailed Samantha.

'Oh, I'll deal with that when it happens,' said Nanny Piggins as she stepped out onto the hose.

'I can't look,' said Samantha, hiding her face in Boris' fur.

'Don't worry,' said Boris. 'There's no way Nanny Piggins would fall on the way to getting a slice of cake.'

'She wouldn't?' asked Samantha hopefully.

'No,' said Boris, 'although she might fall on the way back if she was too busy licking her fingers.'

'Quick, Nigel,' called the editor. 'Fetch the photographer. We'll need pictures of this.'

'For the newspaper?' asked Derrick.

'No, in case she falls,' explained the editor. 'For occupational health and safety.'

But they need not have feared. Nanny Piggins progressed slowly but confidently across the hose. Despite the gale-force gusts of wind, screams of horror from pedestrians below and being hit in the head by a chocolate bar that Boris had thrown at her as encouragement, she soon made it to the other side.

Everyone cheered.

'Clear the front page!' yelled the editor, finally snapping out of his calorie-induced stupor. 'We've got a new lead story!'

'What's the headline?' asked the senior copy editor. 'High Wire Hog Heroics?'

'No,' said the editor. 'Potty Pig Defies Death.'

Meanwhile in the building opposite, Nanny Piggins was having a lovely time leading the office workers in the singing of Happy Birthday and cutting up the cake herself to make sure that everybody, especially Melanie from accounts (the birthday girl) got a really big slice.

Unfortunately, at that moment Nanny Piggins' luck turned. The wonderful adrenalin-induced hysteria of the impromptu party was ruined by a team of police officers bursting into the break room and telling Nanny Piggins she was under arrest.

And so a few short hours later Nanny Piggins, Boris and the children were sitting outside a courtroom waiting for Nanny Piggins' case to come up before the local magistrate. Nanny Piggins was using the opportunity to practise.

'This is ridiculous!' yelled Nanny Piggins. 'It's a miscarriage of justice!'

'You're not going to say that to the judge, are you?' asked Derrick.

'The Police Sergeant did warn you that he was going on a two-week holiday,' Samantha reminded her, 'and that you should try to stay out of trouble while he was away.'

'But how was I to know that his replacement would be such a stickler for the rules?' protested Nanny Piggins.

'Police officers usually are,' said Michael. 'It's kind of the whole point of their job.'

'Please don't let them send you to jail,' sobbed Boris. 'If you're put away, who is going to brush all the knots out of my fur in those hard-to-reach places?'

'Pish! They're not going to send me to jail!' declared Nanny Piggins. 'I rang Isabella Dunkhurst's office. She's the best courtroom lawyer in the country, plus she can tap dance (for further information, see Chapter 1 of *Nanny Piggins and the Accidental Blast-off*), so I'm sure she'll have us home in time to watch *The Young and the Irritable*.'

'Ahem.' A man behind them pretended to cough to get their attention. 'I'm afraid Ms Dunkhurst could not be here today.'

Nanny Piggins, Boris and the children turned to see a very pompous but smartly dressed man, with slicked-back hair and a self-important air about him.

'Who are you?' asked Nanny Piggins rudely. She did not care for men who put more oil on their hair than their salad dressing.

'My name is Montgomery St John,' explained Montgomery St John. 'Ms Dunkhurst is touring Central Africa with her little dancing show at the moment. Apparently she has a large fan base in Botswana, but she left strict instructions about what to do if you should call and need legal help.'

'She did?' asked Nanny Piggins. 'But how did she think that sending a pompous man with greasy hair would help me?'

'I am the firm's leading barrister,' said Montgomery. 'I have not lost a case in nine years. Rest assured I won't have any trouble getting you out of this little difficulty.'

'Why did you lose nine years ago?' asked Nanny Piggins shrewdly.

'What?' asked Montgomery. He clearly had not been expecting this question.

'Why did you lose the last case you lost?' asked Nanny Piggins again.

'Oh, there wasn't anything wrong with my arguments,' said Montgomery.

'Then what happened?' pushed Nanny Piggins.

Montgomery was starting to look a little embarrassed. 'I had a cold and I kept sneezing when I should have been saying "Objection!"'

'Hmm,' said Nanny Piggins. 'Then I suppose you'll do, as long as we keep plenty of antihistamines handy.'

'The People vs Piggins,' called the bailiff.

'That's us,' said Montgomery. 'We'd better go in.'

They all filed into the courtroom.

'What defence are you going to use?' Derrick asked Montgomery.

'Temporary insanity,' said Montgomery. 'I'll tell the judge that she is a pig and that the smell of cake makes her insane.'

'What?!' exploded Nanny Piggins. 'You'll say no such thing! The smell of cake does not make anybody insane. On the contrary, it makes you more sane. It puts everything in perspective and makes sense of the world. One whiff of that buttery cocoa-laden bliss and instantly you know there is nothing more important in the entire universe than putting that in your mouth.'

'Yes yes, you can say that when they put you on the stand,' encouraged Montgomery. 'It will support my argument nicely.'

'Hold my handbag,' Nanny Piggins said to Samantha. 'I'm going to bite him.'

Fortunately for the trouser legs of Montgomery

St John's Armani suit, Nanny Piggins never got the opportunity to bite him because at that very moment the bailiff called out, 'All rise for the Honourable Judge Birchmore.'

Everyone stood up, except Montgomery. He went very pale and started to shake. 'That bailiff didn't say Judge Birchmore, did he? Perhaps he said Judge Darmon or Judge Hsu?'

'No, he definitely said Birchmore,' Michael assured him.

'Oh no!' said Montgomery, beginning to tremble.

'What's wrong?' asked Michael.

'She's awful,' whispered Montgomery. 'She's so mean to everyone. The only reason I got to be senior defence counsel at our firm is because she made the last two senior defence counsels cry and quit the law forever.'

'What did she do to them?' asked Nanny Piggins.

'Make rude comments about their weight?' guessed Boris. (That always reduced him to tears.)

'Or force them to do extra maths homework,' guessed Michael. (That would certainly break his spirit.)

'No, she was just plain mean,' shuddered Montgomery. 'The way she can yell and scream at a lawyer is horrifying. I don't know how she does it. I think it involves circular breathing and excellent voice projection.'

Just then there was a shuffle of movement behind the magistrate's desk.

'She's coming,' said Michael.

'You'll have to excuse me a moment,' said Montgomery. 'I left my chapstick in the car.'

'What?' protested Nanny Piggins.

But Montgomery St John had already sprinted out of the courtroom.

'He is coming back, isn't he?' worried Samantha.

'Of course,' said Nanny Piggins. 'He's a professional lawyer. He can't just run away from the courtroom.'

Unfortunately Nanny Piggins' words were immediately contradicted by what they all saw out the courtroom window. They saw Montgomery run to his expensive Italian sports car, jump in and speed away.

'He said he left the chapstick in his car, not his house, didn't he?' said Nanny Piggins.

'Silence in the court,' called the bailiff.

They turned and looked at Judge Birchmore. She seemed harmless enough to the children. She was a small wizened old lady of at least 75, perhaps even 80 years old. But Nanny Piggins was not so confident. 'I don't like this,' she whispered.

'You're worried because your defence lawyer just ran away,' guessed Michael.

'No, I'm worried that the judge is so thin,' said Nanny Piggins. 'She clearly hasn't had a slice of cake in decades. And if she doesn't eat cake, how can I bribe her?'

Judge Birchmore looked up from her papers and peered out at the courtroom, her gaze resting on Boris. 'Why is that bear crying?' she demanded.

Nanny Piggins stood up. 'Because he is worried that I may be sent to jail, your Justiceness.'

Judge Birchmore peered over her glasses at Nanny Piggins. 'Well *he'll* be sent to jail himself if he doesn't stop blubbering in my courtroom.'

'Michael, perhaps you'd better take Boris outside,' said Nanny Piggins. 'Being Russian, I don't think he is capable of going through a whole court case without crying. And I don't think prison food would agree with him. I doubt they would supply bear-sized portions.'

Michael led the weeping Boris away.

'Where's your lawyer?' demanded Judge Birchmore.

'He ran away,' said Nanny Piggins truthfully.

'Hmm,' said Judge Birchmore reading over her papers. 'Given the litany of charges against you, that seems only sensible.'

'Don't worry, your Honourableness, I am fully prepared to defend myself,' said Nanny Piggins confidently.

Judge Birchmore peered over her glasses again. 'Really?' she asked, smiling the way a crocodile might smile just before it bites off your leg. 'You are aware of the saying that anyone who defends themself has a fool for a client?'

'Well that wouldn't be true in my case, would it?' said Nanny Piggins, 'because clearly I'm not a fool, I'm a pig.'

'Yes, well I've reviewed your case. It seems like a fairly simple matter of recklessly endangering the public, needlessly causing panic and violently trying to bite the shins of three separate policemen,' said Judge Birchmore.

'In my defence,' interrupted Nanny Piggins, 'my mouth was so full of cake, even if I had been able to get hold of their legs, I don't think I could have fit their shins in my mouth.'

'Do not interrupt me when I am telling you off!' snapped Judge Birchmore.

'I thought as defence attorney I was meant to defend myself,' protested Nanny Piggins.

'Only when I say so,' yelled Judge Birchmore so loudly that everyone in the courtroom flinched. (It was really extraordinary that such a small and wizened woman could generate such a loud and unpleasant noise.)

'Then that isn't much of a defence, is it?' argued Nanny Piggins. 'In boxing, if someone hits you you're allowed to hit them straight back. You don't have to wait until they finish and tell you it's your turn.'

'This is not a boxing match!' hollered Judge Birchmore.

'I wish it was,' muttered Nanny Piggins. 'I know who would win.'

'I've never heard such insolence!' exclaimed Judge Birchmore.

'Then you obviously haven't been listening properly,' said Nanny Piggins.

'I was going to let you off with a warning,' screamed Judge Birchmore, 'but now I'm going to give you one hundred hours community service!'

'But you haven't let Nanny Piggins present her defence yet!' protested Derrick.

'Haven't I?' Judge Birchmore looked at the bailiff.

The bailiff looked intimidated, but he was a brave man, having been in the marines for twenty years, so he found the courage to shake his head ever so slightly.

'Very well,' said Judge Birchmore. 'What's your defence?'

'My defence against the charge of public endangerment is that it is all a load of piffle,' stated Nanny Piggins.

'That is not a proper legal argument!' berated Judge Birchmore.

'But it's the truth,' Nanny Piggins assured her. 'I am an international circus megastar. There's no way I'd ever fall off a tightrope onto the heads of the crowd beneath and crush them to death, no matter how windy it was. Especially not when there was a delicious chocolate cream cake to be eaten.'

'The deliciousness of the cake is immaterial to this court case,' yelled Judge Birchmore.

'You only say that because you didn't get a slice,' argued Nanny Piggins. 'If you let me whip up a replica cake I'm sure I can convince you otherwise.'

'Just get on with your argument!' screamed Judge Birchmore.

'Do you think the judge is so cranky because

she is worried she'll miss *The Young and the Irritable* too?' wondered Derrick.

'My defence against the charge of resisting arrest,' continued Nanny Piggins, 'is that the police really should be thanking me for the opportunity I gave them. Arresting an elite athlete like me actually proved to be an invaluable training exercise for the officers involved, and a much better use of their time than hanging out in the doughnut shop chatting up the cashier, which I happen to know was all they were doing at the time, because I saw them when I was up on the tightrope.'

The police officers, who were sitting in court waiting to give evidence, all blushed. They had indeed been in the doughnut shop, but it was not their fault. There is something universal about wearing a blue uniform that makes a person crave deep fried, jam-filled cake.

'All right, I've heard enough!' shrieked Judge Birchmore. 'I sentence you to 200 hours community service.'

'I know maths isn't my strong suit,' said Nanny Piggins, 'but didn't that figure just go up?'

The children nodded.

'But that's unfair!' protested Nanny Piggins. 'All I did was walk across a hose pipe and eat a slice of cake. Since when is that a crime?'

'Since I said it is!' yelled Judge Birchmore, 'and I'm adding contempt of court to your list of misdemeanours! So that's 300 hours community service.'

'I don't have contempt for the court!' declared Nanny Piggins. 'I only have contempt for you!'

Everyone in the room gasped.

'You obviously have no idea how to bake a cake yourself,' continued Nanny Piggins, 'or you wouldn't be so short and skinny.'

Judge Birchmore was now shaking with rage. 'That's it!' she declared. 'I am giving you five thousand hours community service!'

Now everyone in the courtroom gasped. Even the blushing police officers. They had actually quite enjoyed arresting Nanny Piggins. It was much more exciting than telling off shoplifters or giving out speeding tickets. They did not want to see her get in that much trouble.

But the Judge's decision was final. She slammed her gavel onto her desk.

Fortunately for Nanny Piggins, Judge Birchmore immediately got up and turned to leave the room so she did not see Nanny Piggins lunge across the court in a last minute attempt to bite her scrawny shins, or that it took all three children, Boris and the bailiff to drag her out of the courtroom.

'At least she didn't send you to jail,' said Samantha later that afternoon, as they all sat around their kitchen table feeling gloomy.

'Hah!' said Nanny Piggins. 'A jail sentence is nothing! You're forgetting I escaped from the circus. So it would take much more than a twelve-foot-high electrified cyclone fence and guards with machine guns to hold me.'

'But what about the community service?' said Michael. 'Five thousand hours is a lot. Even if you worked ten hours a day it would still take you a year and a half. How will you find time to look after us?'

'You don't suppose there's any chance the judge might just forget about it all?' asked Nanny Piggins, looking a little worried.

They all shook their heads sadly. Nanny Piggins looked depressed. But then she put a very large slice of cake in her mouth, and you could almost see the chemical transformation it had on her body. She sat up straight, colour returned to her cheeks and a sparkle to her eye. She licked the icing off her trotters. 'Piffle!' said Nanny Piggins. 'I'm sure it will all work out. These things always do. Terrible things are never as bad as you think they are going to be. Except for carrot cake. That is always atrocious. As long as they don't expect me to eat carrot cake, I'm sure this community service will fly by.'

The children were not so confident. They loved their nanny very much. But seeing sense was not her strong suit. So they suspected that the following months would not be easy at all.

CHAPTER 2

Nanny Piggins and the Ridiculous Imposter

'Now this is the incredibly dangerous stage!' whispered Nanny Piggins. 'Is everyone wearing their protective gear?'

The children nodded. They were all wearing cricket gloves and swimming goggles as they peered over Nanny Piggins' shoulder and watched the brown liquid she was stirring start to bubble.

'It doesn't look very dangerous,' said Michael dubiously.

'That is exactly why it is so hazardous,' said Nanny Piggins. 'You think, because fudge is so wonderfully delicious, what harm could such a scrumptious treat do, don't you?'

The children nodded.

'That is exactly how fudge lures you into a false sense of security!' declared Nanny Piggins. 'While set fudge is wonderful, yummy happiness in a lump, cooking fudge is seriously unsafe! Molten sugar is both super boiling hot and super sticky on your skin. So it doesn't just burn you, it keeps burning you while you run around the kitchen howling, "Get it off, get it off, get it off!"'

'The army could use hot fudge as a weapon,' suggested Michael.

'They did!' said Nanny Piggins, 'but they had to stop because it caused such terrible burns.'

'But surely that's what they wanted?' said Derrick.

'The fudge didn't burn the enemy,' said Nanny Piggins. 'It burnt the soldiers using it because they couldn't resist licking the delicious fudge and they got terrible burns on their tongues.'

'Really?' said Derrick.

'Yes, the dangers of fudge would be more widely known except, like so many military secrets, the truth remains classified,' said Nanny Piggins.

'So how can we tell when it's ready?' asked Samantha.

'By the ploppiness of the bubbles,' said Nanny Piggins.

The children all peered into the pot again. The bubbling fudge looked like any bubbling liquid to them. But they didn't like to say so in case this led to a three-hour lecture on comparative ploppiness. (Derrick had made the mistake of questioning Nanny Piggins' opinion on the runniness of honey once, and he could now write a book on the viscosity of bee-regurgitated nectar as a result of all the information his nanny had forced him to learn to cure his lamentable ignorance.)

'As the fudge gets hotter and more moisture evaporates,' explained Nanny Piggins, 'it becomes thicker and the bubbles don't pop open like water bubbles, they plop and flop like fudge bubbles. Then you know it's ready and it is time to start testing the fudge.'

'By eating some?' asked Michael hopefully.

'Of course not!' exclaimed Nanny Piggins. 'Do you want to get horrible fourth-degree burns to your tongue like those poor soldiers?'

Michael did not.

'No, you get a saucer of cold tap water,'

continued Nanny Piggins, 'then drop one drop of the boiling fudge into the water. If it immediately sets and becomes hard to the touch, the fudge is ready.'

'Then can you taste it?' asked Derrick.

Nanny Piggins sighed. 'Samantha, fetch your brother a chocolate bar. He is clearly becoming delirious with fudge longing.'

But Samantha did not hear her nanny. She was too busy staring at the boiling fudge. (Samantha had a flashlight strapped to her head for maximum analysis of the liquid.) 'Nanny Piggins!' she exclaimed. 'The fudge! It's starting to plop!'

'It's time!' yelled Nanny Piggins. 'Quick, fetch me a saucer of water. We mustn't dillydally; the window of fudge perfection is a short one.'

Michael rushed over with a saucer of cold water. He was getting good at running with containers of liquid, so he only spilled half of it on the floor.

Nanny Piggins put the saucer on the countertop and carefully, using a teaspoon, scooped the smallest portion out of the pot.

'Couldn't you just use a cooking thermometer?' asked Derrick. 'Samson Wallace says that's what Nanny Anne uses.'

Nanny Piggins paused and glared at Derrick out

of the corner of her eye. (Nanny Anne was Nanny Piggins' arch nemesis. To be strictly accurate, one of her arch-nemeses. She had quite a few, but Nanny Anne was definitely in the top three. She was a woman so puritanically obsessed with hygiene that she often gave poor Samson Wallace soap sandwiches in his lunch box, just in case he was thinking of saying something naughty.)

'Sorry,' said Derrick. 'I'll fetch myself a chocolate bar. I'm obviously not thinking straight.'

Nanny Piggins returned her concentration to her half-teaspoon of fudge. She held the precious confectionary over the saucer and dropped the brown liquid in. Everyone leaned forward for a closer look. The fudge had not flattened or gone runny. It had formed a nice round mound.'

'Excellent,' muttered Nanny Piggins. 'Pass me the wooden spoon, please.'

Michael handed her a wooden spoon.

Using the handle, Nanny Piggins slowly and carefully prodded the lump of fudge. The brown mixture crumpled slightly but still stayed in one piece.

'Perfect!' whispered Nanny Piggins. 'We have made the perfect vanilla fudge.'

DING-DONG!

'I thought I told you to disconnect the doorbell,' said Nanny Piggins.

'I did,' protested Derrick. 'It's Father. You disconnect the doorbell so often that he has taken to secretly installing back-up doorbells.'

'Why?' asked Nanny Piggins.

'Because he doesn't like to miss it when salesmen or market researchers come to the door,' explained Derrick. 'He likes rudely telling them to go away.'

'It's the only social contact he has with real people,' added Samantha.

DING-DONG DING-DONG DING-DONG!

'Do you want me to tell them to go away?' asked Michael.

'No,' said Nanny Piggins, putting down her wooden spoon. 'Your father and I do have one thing in common. Rudely telling people to leave is something I enjoy too.'

She marched to the front door, the children following close behind in case they needed to grab her and prevent her from adding to her newly established criminal record.

Nanny Piggins flung open the front door, drawing breath as she did, so she could immediately launch into her tirade. But when she saw who it was on the doorstep, she paused. It was the editor from the newspaper and the girl cadet journalist (who looked much too small for her oversized notepad).

'What are you doing here?' demanded Nanny Piggins. 'Have you come to apologise for not helping defend me in court, when it was the lack of a rope bridge between your office and the adjacent building that forced me to engage in apparently illegal tight-rope walking in the first place?'

'Um . . .' said the editor. 'No.'

'Then give me one good reason why I should not slam this door in your face right now,' demanded Nanny Piggins.

The editor eyed the door warily. 'We're here strictly for professional reasons, nothing to do with your legal problems.'

'Which your negligent building design caused,' said Nanny Piggins petulantly.

'Hmmm,' said the editor, not wanting to agree (for legal reasons) but too frightened to disagree. 'Anyway, the real reason we're here is because we want a quote for a story about something else entirely.'

'Ahhh,' said Nanny Piggins. 'You want my opinion about the mayor's dress sense. Well I think it is dreadful. You can quote me on that. And Piggins is spelled P-I-G-G-I-N-S.'

'No,' said the editor. 'Although we will make a note of it.'

The young journalist nodded and scrawled in shorthand furiously.

'We're here because there is a new pig in town, on a speaking tour to promote his book,' explained the editor. 'It is a very exciting book in which he tells the story of all his amazing feats and accomplishments.'

'What's that got to do with me?' asked Nanny Piggins suspiciously.

'Well,' continued the editor. 'Among the many achievements listed in his book, he describes, in great detail, how he became "The World's Greatest Flying Pig".'

'What?! WHAT!! WHATTT!!!!' yelled Nanny Piggins.

The editor and the cadet journalist took several steps back.

'He says he is "The World's Greatest Flying Pig",' repeated the editor, as he turned, ready to run in case Nanny Piggins took after him.

'Who would dare utter such a lie?' asked Nanny Piggins.

'Eduardo the flying armadillo?' suggested Derrick.

'No,' said Nanny Piggins. 'True, he was deluded enough to think he was the world's greatest flying animal. But he never claimed to be a pig. He seemed very proud of his armadillo heritage.'

'Perhaps it's one of your identical fourteenuplet sisters,' suggested Samantha. 'Several of them are evil.'

'Yes,' agreed Nanny Piggins, 'but they are all brilliantly evil in their own right. They'd have no need to steal credit for my accomplishments.'

'He's also claiming –,' said the cadet journalist, reading from her notes – 'to be the first pig to climb Mount Everest, the first pig to win the Nobel Prize, the first pig in space, the greatest pig international super-spy, the greatest pig international jewel thief . . .'

'But that is a list of all my sisters' and my achieve-ments,' interrupted Nanny Piggins. 'Who would be stupid enough to claim such an unbelievable litany of things?'

'An egomaniac?' suggested Derrick.

'An attention seeker?' suggested Samantha.

'A delusional egomaniacal attention seeker?' suggested Michael.

'Or,' said Nanny Piggins, 'no, it can't be. Not my idiot older brother, Bramwell?'

'Yes, that's him,' agreed the editor. 'Bramwell Piggins. In his book, he claims he has allowed his sisters to get credit for his achievements to help boost their self-esteem.'

'I'll boost his self-esteem when I see him,' muttered Nanny Piggins, 'by giving him a good hard whack on the –'

'Nanny Piggins! The fudge!' yelped Samantha, suddenly reminding them all of the much more important matter in the kitchen.

When they returned to the stove (the editor and the young journalist came with them in case something newsworthy had happened. And indeed it had), the fudge was a sorry mess. It had now boiled down entirely and the wooden spoon was set hard in the blackened mass at the bottom of the pot.

Nanny Piggins burst into tears.

'Don't cry,' pleaded Samantha. 'I'm sure your brother didn't mean to betray you.'

'I'm not crying about that,' sniffed Nanny Piggins. 'I'm crying about the fudge. Now I'll have to go to the shop and buy some.'

'Among his other claims,' said the editor, 'Bramwell Piggins also says he is the world's greatest fudge maker.'

'Right, that's it,' said Nanny Piggins. 'My older brother needs to be taught a lesson.'

'He's signing his book at the local bookshop tomorrow,' smiled the editor. 'We'll send a photographer if you're turning up.'

'Send two,' said Nanny Piggins ominously.

At five minutes to nine the next morning, Nanny Piggins and the children were sitting in the front row of their local bookshop waiting for Bramwell to arrive for his book signing. Nanny Piggins glowered at a large promotional poster for Bramwell's book, which read:

The Adventures of Bramwell Piggins
(World's Greatest All-Round Pig)
Volume One

A full night of thinking about her brother's wicked treachery had only made Nanny Piggins madder. And while she looked even more beautiful and glamorous than usual in her knee-length designer dress and bejewelled headband, the children knew she had her hot pink wrestling leotard on underneath.

'Nanny Piggins?' asked Samantha carefully (she did not want her nanny to launch into a premature rage). 'Why did you never mention that you had a brother? We've always known about your identical fourteenuplet sisters, but in the whole time we've known you you've never mentioned Bramwell before.'

'You wouldn't understand,' said Nanny Piggins, 'because you have two perfectly lovely brothers. But trust me, if you had a brother like Bramwell, you'd do your best to forget he existed as well.'

'Is he evil?' asked Derrick.

'Hah!' snorted Nanny Piggins. 'He isn't interesting enough to be evil. He's just so . . . so . . . I don't think there is a word for him – pathetic, annoying, inadequate, whining, ungrateful, blubbering, waste-of-space – none of them quite covers it.'

'What does he do that's so awful?' asked Michael.

'That's just it,' explained Nanny Piggins. 'He does nothing! All my sisters, even the evil ones, have a considerable work ethic and dedication to principles. Wendy may be a villainous international super-spy but she has worked hard and she is a very talented villainous super-spy. Anthea may be an incurable jewel thief but her dedication to apricot danishes rivals Mother Theresa's dedication to the poor. And even Katerina, with her insatiable love of vegetables, even *she* has an admirable work ethic, getting up at 4 am every day to water her zucchinis. But Bramwell – he does nothing. He gloms from one job to the next, being fired for incompetence, gluttony and oversleeping. And to make matters worse, when he is between jobs he goes around claiming to be a . . . a . . . I can't say it, it's too mortifying.'

'A terrorist?' asked Derrick.

'Worse,' said Nanny Piggins.

'A used car salesman?' guessed Michael.

'Much worse,' said Nanny Piggins, hiding her face in shame.

'A truancy officer?' guessed Samantha.

'No,' whispered Nanny Piggins, dabbing away tears of shame. 'He tells people he is a . . . poet.'

'No!' exclaimed all three horrified children.

Nanny Piggins nodded her head and closed her eyes tight, trying to block out the disgrace. 'He even tries to read his poetry to you if you can't run away from him because you've broken your ankle or got your foot caught in a giant clam.'

'No wonder you try so hard to disown him,' said Samantha, giving her nanny a supportive hug.

Just then a long limousine pulled up outside the shop.

'He's here!' exclaimed Derrick.

An anxious publicist rushed over to open the passenger door. The children were shocked to see Bramwell for the first time. They had assumed he would look like his sisters, but he did not. True, his facial features were similar, but there was one shocking dissimilarity. Bramwell was enormously fat. All Nanny Piggins' sisters were extremely lean and athletic. But Bramwell was as round as he was tall. Admittedly, like his sisters he was only four foot tall, but still it was unusual to see someone who was also four foot wide.

'Oh yes, I forgot to mention,' said Nanny Piggins. 'That is the other shameful thing about Bramwell – he has a slight weight problem. Now, as you know, I am not normally one to judge a person for that. Eating is such a priority. But in Bramwell's case, he is a pig, and it is such a cliché for a pig to be as fat as a pig.'

Bramwell waddled across the store, smiling smugly and posing for photographs as he was waylaid by fans. Eventually he made his way to the front, and with the help of a good hard shove from his publicist, he managed to climb up onto the podium.

'Good morning,' said Bramwell, smiling down at his audience. 'It is wonderful to see your adoring faces.'

The audience clapped.

'And ladies, no marriage proposals please,' smirked Bramwell. 'At least not until after my speech.'

The women in the audience giggled.

Bramwell took out his notes, winked at the audience, cleared his throat and began his speech. 'People are always asking me, Bramwell Piggins, how did you come to be so wonderful at everything? Adventurer, inventor, medical breakthrougher, heroic rescuer, pastry chef extraordinaire . . . Does your talent know no bounds? And I'm afraid the simple answer is "no". Even as a young piglet, my little sisters would sit and watch in awe as I explained particle physics, demonstrated jujitsu or whipped up a delicious batch of authentic Lebanese baklava. Obviously it was too much for them to ever emulate. But in their own simple way they enjoyed watching me be brilliant.'

Nanny Piggins could bear it no longer. 'Stop it!' she shrieked. 'Stop it at once before I am sick all over this cheap synthetic carpet.'

Bramwell peered over the edge of his podium. He was too fat to see the front row, so he could not see who was yelling at him.

'You should be thoroughly ashamed of yourself!'

denounced Nanny Piggins. 'If Mother were alive today she would sit on you to teach you a lesson about stealing better people's identities.'

'Mother?' yelped Bramwell. 'She's not here, is she?' He looked about in a panic.

'Of course not, you twit,' condemned Nanny Piggins. 'She's been dead for years.'

Bramwell heaved a sigh of relief. 'Oh yes, of course, thank goodness.'

Nanny Piggins was now shaking with rage. 'Leaving aside your pleasure in our mother's death – I shall bite you for that later – first things first, how dare you steal my identity and the accomplishments of all our sisters just to flatter your own ego and sell books!'

'Sarah? Is that you?' asked Bramwell. While his fourteen sisters were physically identical, from much experience Bramwell was able to identify them by their own unique way of yelling at him.

'It certainly is,' said Nanny Piggins. 'And how dare you come to my home town claiming to be "The World's Greatest Flying Pig".'

'I didn't know you lived here,' protested Bramwell.

'Balderdash!' exclaimed Nanny Piggins. 'When you drive into town there is a great big sign saying

"Welcome to Dullsford. Population 66,782. Home of Nanny Piggins, World's Greatest Flying Pig."'

'In his defence,' whispered Derrick, 'the last bit is hard to read because it is in Boris' handwriting.'

'There is no excuse!' yelled Nanny Piggins. 'How dare you, who have achieved so little, take the credit for we who have done so much.'

Bramwell winked at his audience. 'You'll have to excuse my little sister. Her imagination runs away with her from time to time.'

'What?!' exclaimed Nanny Piggins.

'Don't judge her,' continued Bramwell (while surreptitiously trying to shove copies of his own books into his socks for protection). 'It is hard for a tiny sapling to grow in the shadow of a great oak.'

'Did he just patronise me?' exclaimed Nanny Piggins. 'Right, that's it. I'm taking my frock off. It's shin-biting time.'

'Sarah, my dear,' said Bramwell, clutching the podium tightly and keeping it between him and his sister. 'There is no need for that.'

'Then immediately admit that your whole book is just a pack of lies,' demanded Nanny Piggins.

Bramwell paused. He thought about how much he liked getting great big royalty cheques from his publisher, and then he thought about how a few shin bites would soon heal and go away. 'No I won't,' said Bramwell. 'Every single word is true and you can't prove otherwise.'

The audience cheered. Bramwell looked proud of his cleverness.

But Nanny Piggins was baffled by his stupidity. 'Of course I can prove you're a fraud, you great big idiot. Nothing would be easier. For a start I can show that I am the world's greatest flying pig by challenging you to a dual. Right here tomorrow morning, let's both get blasted out of cannons and see who flies further. That'll soon settle that.'

'What a brilliant idea!' exclaimed the publicist, who got out her mobile phone so she could tell all her journalist friends.

'Now hang on,' protested Bramwell. 'I am an author now. Um . . . it would be unseemly and . . . er . . . besides, I don't have a cannon.'

'Don't worry,' said the publicist. 'I'll arrange it all. Publicity like this is unbeatable. Your books will fly off the shelves.'

'Good, it's settled then,' said Nanny Piggins. 'Prepare to be belittled right here tomorrow morning at 9 am.'

Nanny Piggins then grabbed hold of her brother,

gave him a noogie, a wedgie, a wet willy and several other physically unpleasant things siblings do to each other, before storming out of the bookshop with the children. The audience again clapped. They had expected a rather dull book reading, but instead they had apparently been treated to a dramatic morning of improvised theatre.

During the night Nanny Piggins and Boris went down to the local war museum and borrowed the largest Howitzer. (The war museum had become used to this and in fact had given Nanny Piggins her own key so she would not disturb the security guard's nap schedule.)

Nanny Piggins then had a brief but thorough training workout, eating 50 pounds of chocolate-covered caramels to increase her density and therefore velocity through the air.

At nine o'clock the next morning she arrived at the bookshop in her favourite suede lemon-coloured body suit (with black and red stripes), as Boris pulled her 25-tonne cannon into position. There was a huge crowd already gathered to watch the display.

'We're here!' announced Nanny Piggins. 'Now where is that good-for-nothing Bramwell so we can get started?'

'He's right here,' said the publicist, turning round to point at . . . an empty space.

'Where?' asked Samantha.

'But he was right here a second ago,' protested the publicist.

Nanny Piggins looked at Derrick's watch. It ticked over from 9.00 to 9.01. 'Of course,' she said, 'he's not coming back.'

'But surely not,' panicked the publicist. 'Look at the crowd. He can't let them down. Some of them have pre-bought books, expecting him to sign them.'

'Well, I must confess I have underestimated my brother,' admitted Nanny Piggins. 'In my haste to condemn him for stealing credit for the talents of his sisters, I had forgotten his one great talent.'

'He has a great talent?' asked Derrick.

'He is a Piggins,' Nanny Piggins reminded them. 'So yes, he does have one extraordinary ability.'

'What is it?' asked the publicist optimistically. 'I hope it sells books.'

'He has a unique and unparalleled talent for running away from angry people,' said Nanny Piggins.

'Is that a talent?' asked Samantha.

'Oh yes,' said Nanny Piggins. 'Think about it.

If you were so inadequate and your sisters were so brilliant and you had a tendency to claim credit for their accomplishments, you'd learn to be good at running away too.'

'But Nanny Piggins, how can he run when he's so . . .' Derrick did not like to say the word.

'Fat?' supplied Nanny Piggins. 'Yes, I know. But he is still a pig and therefore a gifted athlete compared to a mere human. Plus he somehow manages to use his greater weight to his advantage by doing lots of plunging, plummeting and sinking when he is on the run.'

'So that's it?' asked Samantha. 'It's all over?'

'Not at all,' said Nanny Piggins. 'Now we have to find him and punish him.'

'But how?' asked Derrick.

'Luckily I had the foresight to bake a GPS tracking device into a shortbread cookie that I slipped into my brother's pocket yesterday while I was giving him a noogie,' said Nanny Piggins.

'Could you bake me a whole batch of those cookies so I can keep track of all my authors?' asked the publicist.

Nanny Piggins retrieved a handheld radar device from the pocket of her dress. (She had broken the heart of many a European designer by insisting they include pockets in their couture frocks.) She switched it on and a green blip appeared on the screen. 'That's him!' exclaimed Nanny Piggins. 'Bramwell is the green blip. Follow me.'

And so Nanny Piggins followed the blip, the children and the publicist followed Nanny Piggins and the crowd of Bramwell fans followed them all, determined to get their books signed.

They tracked Bramwell down the road, over a fence (or more accurately through a fence, which had collapsed when Bramwell tried to climb it), along a wall, under shrubbery, out onto another road, into a cake shop (with particularly delicious lamingtons) and down an alley, where they reached a dead end.

'Do you think he climbed one of these buildings?' asked Samantha, looking up at the six-storey walls surrounding them on three sides.

Nanny Piggins looked at her monitor and the blip clearly moving away from them. 'No,' she said. 'When you have the physique of my brother you never go up when you could go down.'

They all looked at Nanny Piggins' feet. She was standing on a manhole.

'Into the sewers?' asked Derrick. 'But that's disgusting.'

'As is my brother,' said Nanny Piggins sadly.

'It's so unhygienic,' said Samantha.

'And stinky,' added Michael.

'My brother is no stranger to stink,' revealed Nanny Piggins. 'He once went an entire calendar year without taking a bath.'

'What happened?' asked Derrick. (He had long wondered what would happen if he never took a bath, aside from having much more time to read comics.)

'The stench became so unbearable that my sister Wendy waited until he was asleep, taped a high-powered hose to the inside of his trouser leg, then turned the hose on,' remembered Nanny Piggins. 'He was blasted with water from the inside out. Eventually his clothes swelled up with the pressurised water until they exploded off and he was left clean as a whistle.'

'I bet that taught him a lesson,' said Samantha.

'No, actually it taught Wendy a lesson. Because then Bramwell didn't go and buy new clothes for three weeks,' said Nanny Piggins, 'and the only thing worse than a stinky brother is a naked brother.'

'So are you going to let him disappear into the sewers?' asked Michael.

'Of course not,' said Nanny Piggins. 'I brought a bag of marshmallows in anticipation of precisely this eventuality.'

'How will eating marshmallows help?' asked Derrick.

'I'm not going to eat them,' said Nanny Piggins. 'I'm going to shove them up my nose, and I suggest you do the same if you are coming with me.' And with that Nanny Piggins shoved two pink marshmallows into her snout and heaved the manhole cover aside. As the first wave of stench wafted up, the children and Boris hastily shoved marshmallows into their own noses. The crowd of Bramwell fans backed away, realising they did not want their books signed by someone who would willingly climb down into that odour. Only the publicist lunged forward, catching Nanny Piggins by the sleeve.

'Before you go,' said the publicist, 'is there any chance I could sign you to a multi-book deal? Because if your brother does prove to be a huge fraud and we have to pulp all his books for legal reasons, we will be looking to sign a new pig adventurer.'

'Me write books!' scoffed Nanny Piggins. 'Don't be ridiculous! I'm far too busy having adventures to waste my time writing about them.'

'But we could get you a ghost writer,' argued the publicist.

'I absolutely refuse to work with ghosts,' said Nanny Piggins. 'Just because they are trapped for eternity between worlds doesn't give them the right to go around waking people up with their wailing.'

And with that she disappeared down into the black stinking hole.

The sewers turned out to be every bit as unpleasant as you might imagine. They were smelly, slimy and wet. The absolute last place you should go if you happened to be wearing a suede, lemon-coloured bodysuit. But Nanny Piggins was on a mission and therefore heedless of her appearance.

'This way,' she whispered. (You should always whisper in a sewer so as not to attract the attention of the rats.) They set off following the blip, only now they moved more slowly and cautiously. (The sewer is one place you really do not want to fall over.)

As the morning wore on they got closer and closer to the blip. Bramwell actually moved quicker than his sister, because he dived into the sewers like they were waterslides, slipping and sliding from one tunnel to the next. But he also stopped to rest all the time and that is how Nanny Piggins and the children gained ground on him.

After several hours they finally had him within reach. 'He's just up ahead,' whispered Nanny Piggins excitedly. 'Down this tunnel and around the bend.'

They crept forward quietly until they got to the corner. Then Nanny Piggins leapt out to confront her brother.

'Aha! There's no escaping now!' she yelled.

But Bramwell was not there.

'Where's he gone?' asked Nanny Piggins, looking down at her monitor. The blip had disappeared.

'Look,' called Derrick. He was pointing to a shower of shortbread cookie crumbs on the floor.

'Oh no,' said Nanny Piggins. 'He found the shortbread cookie and ate it.'

'Won't the tracking device still work in his stomach?' asked Michael.

'I doubt it. Mother taught us to chew all our food 32 times,' said Nanny Piggins forlornly.

And so Nanny Piggins and the children had to abandon their pursuit of Bramwell. They climbed out of the sewers and made their way home. Which was almost as unpleasant as being in the sewers, because everyone they walked past leapt away in horror, or fainted from the stench of their now ruined clothes. Nanny Piggins' beautiful suede bodysuit was certainly not lemon-coloured anymore.

After they got home and had scrubbed themselves vigorously with several bars of soap for a considerable amount of time, Nanny Piggins, Boris and the children gathered in the kitchen to cheer themselves up with a few serves of banoffee pudding (a wonderful confection of banana, toffee and cream that is excellent for restoring spirits).

'Are you terribly disappointed that you didn't catch Bramwell?' Michael asked his nanny.

'Not really,' said Nanny Piggins, between bites. 'I'm sure he'll turn up again some day – posing as someone incredibly glamorous like an astronaut, or a race car driver, or a nanny – and when he does, I'll bite him.' (Eating pudding always made her feel philosophical.)

'I'm exhausted,' said Boris. 'When they built those sewers I don't think they had ten-foot-tall bears in mind. I banged my head so many times.'

'I told you not to do so much leaping in the air,' said Nanny Piggins.

'I can't help it. I'm a ballet dancer,' said Boris. 'I always do a grand jeté when I see a rat.'

Boris took a bucket of honey from the cupboard and trudged out to his shed. The children and Nanny

Piggins were just helping themselves to their seventh servings of banoffee pudding when their munching was interrupted by a bloodcurdling scream.

'Yaaaaaaggghhhhh!'

'That sounded like Boris,' exclaimed Nanny Piggins, leaping to her trotters.

But then there was a second even more blood-curdling scream.

'Wwaaaaaagggghhhhh!' said another screamer.

They all burst out the back door just as Boris burst out of the shed. (Unfortunately he missed the doorway and smashed out a bear-shaped portion of wall.)

'Sarah, save me!' Boris squealed. 'There's someone in my bed.'

'Not that Goldilocks again!' said Nanny Piggins. 'Why won't she leave you poor bears alone and take a nap in her own house for once?'

'I don't think it is Goldilocks this time,' said Boris, 'unless she has gained weight.'

Nanny Piggins and the children peered through the large hole in the shed wall. On Boris' bed they could see an enormous lump, not unlike a huge beach ball covered in a blanket.

'That lump looks familiar,' said Nanny Piggins as she climbed into the shed and picked up a garden trowel. She then gave the lump a sharp whack. And lo and behold her brother leapt up, screaming.

'Bramwell!' exclaimed the children.

'Why on earth would he go to so much trouble to run away from you, only to come here?' marvelled Samantha.

'Because he might have a genius for escape,' said Nanny Piggins, 'but he is still a nitwit.'

'I had nowhere else to go,' blubbered Bramwell, still rubbing his bottom. (Which was not easy because his arms were barely long enough to reach it). 'I spent all my book advance on cupcakes. And no hotel will take me. I have been blacklisted from anywhere that serves a buffet breakfast.'

'But why come here?' asked Derrick.

'I didn't think anyone would notice me in the shed,' said Bramwell.

'Normally that is true,' said Boris. He certainly had gone unnoticed living there for the longest time. And a ten-foot-tall bear is even more eye-catching than a four-foot-wide pig.

'Well, you can't stay here,' said Nanny Piggins. 'You'll just have to go back to your old job.'

'Bramwell has a job?' asked Michael.

'Yes, he is a waste disposal technician at a factory,' said Nanny Piggins.

'He takes out garbage?' asked Derrick.

'Not exactly,' said Nanny Piggins. 'He eats it.'

'What?!' exclaimed the children, thinking that Bramwell was even more unhygienic than they had imagined.

'It's not as bad as it sounds,' explained Nanny Piggins. 'Bramwell works at a chocolate factory, so if someone accidentally ruins a batch of chocolate by burning it, curdling it or adding a coconut filling, Bramwell comes in and cleans it all up. He's a much more environmentally friendly alternative than putting it in landfill.'

'It's not very glamorous though,' sulked Bramwell.

'But you're not very glamorous, are you?' Nanny Piggins pointed out. 'And the sooner you accept that, the happier you'll be. The whole world can't be filled with impossibly glamorous incredibly talented pigs. It would be exhausting. No, there are fourteen of us, and that is just the right number.'

So Nanny Piggins sent Bramwell packing (with twelve large chocolate cakes and a crate of sherbet lemons to sustain him on his bus ride home). And everything returned to normal. Well, almost normal. The publicist did still call twenty times a day begging Nanny Piggins to sign a book deal.

CHAPTER 3

Nanny Piggins and the Angry Old People

'I'm so sorry, Nanny Piggins,' said the probation officer for the forty-seventh time.

'There's no need to apologise,' said Nanny Piggins, while offering him another slice of cake. 'It's not your fault the criminal justice system is so terribly unjust and that Judge Birchmore is a raving psychopath.'

'If only there was some way I could give you community service right here in our office,' lamented the probation officer. 'You could do a little filing, type some letters, or just take a nap. I'd let you do it if I had my way.'

'I know,' said Nanny Piggins, patting his hand kindly, 'but I don't mind going out into the community. And I'm not afraid of hard work.'

'It's true,' agreed Michael. 'Nanny Piggins often stays up all night working on her cake recipes.'

'I can tell,' said the probation officer as he stuffed even more cake into his mouth.

'So do your worst,' said Nanny Piggins. 'Treat me as you would any other law-breaking miscreant. Which part of the community do you want me to serve? I could sniff out bombs for the bomb disposal squad, teach trapeze to school teachers or give a wrestling workshop to the army.'

'Oh, we don't do any community service like that,' said the probation officer. 'I'm afraid what I can offer you is far less glamorous.'

'How much less glamorous?' asked Nanny Piggins.

'The Golden Willows Retirement Home needs a volunteer,' said the probation officer.

'To do what?' asked Nanny Piggins. 'Help the old people re-enact historical scenes from their pasts?'

'No, just talk to them,' said the probation officer. 'The nursing home's television broke down last week. The residents are getting restless. They need someone to go down and talk with them or organise a game of bingo. That sort of thing.'

Nanny Piggins leaned towards Derrick. 'Is bingo that game where you fire rubber darts at police officers, trying to knock their hats off?' she whispered.

'That's what *you* call bingo,' said Derrick. 'But there is another far more boring version of the game.'

'And what are the alternatives to this "talking to old people"?' asked Nanny Piggins. 'Don't you have something that would better use my athletic cannon-blasting skills?'

'Sorry,' said the probation officer. 'I have very strict instructions from Judge Birchmore that I am to give you no alternatives and make you do the worst job available.'

'Talking to old people doesn't sound that bad,' said Samantha.

'No, you wouldn't think so, would you?' agreed the probation officer. 'But I sent five people down to the retirement home last week and they all came away crying. Three of them opted to go to jail rather than complete their community service.'

'Hmm,' said Nanny Piggins. 'Give me the address. I'm sure the old people can't be that difficult. If I can't placate them with my cake baking, I do still have the Howitzer I borrowed from the war museum. I can always try threatening them.'

Forty minutes later, Nanny Piggins, Boris and the children arrived at the old people's home.

'Are you nervous?' asked Michael.

'Not at all,' said Nanny Piggins. 'Sure, old people can be crotchety. And when you help yourself to their boiled lollies they can yell at you for hours while trying to hit you with their walking sticks. But on the bright side, you can always outrun them.'

With that she stepped forward and pressed the doorbell. They then waited for a minute before it became clear that no-one was coming to answer the door. Nanny Piggins pressed the doorbell again and yelled, 'Yoo-hoo, is anyone home? I'm the court-appointed criminal who is being forced to help you!'

But again no-one answered.

'Does this mean we can go home?' asked Boris.

'We've only been here for 75 seconds,' said

Nanny Piggins. 'If we went home now it would take me two thousand years to get through my community service. We'd better just let ourselves in.'

So Nanny Piggins kicked in the front door (entirely knocking it off its hinges) and they all walked inside.

'What is that odour?' asked Nanny Piggins as she sniffed about. 'It smells like someone is growing mushrooms in here.'

'And why is it so warm?' asked Boris. 'Is this a nursing home for old people who want to pretend they're living in the tropics?'

'I think old people like things to be warm,' explained Samantha. 'It's got something to do with them having bad circulation.'

'Packing them into a mouldy sauna isn't going to help that,' said Nanny Piggins, throwing open a few windows to let in the fresh air. 'The only way to improve circulation is by circulating, preferably down the road to the bakery. A couple of dozen chocolate brownies always get my blood flowing.'

Just then a cleaning woman edged backwards into the room, wiping the floor with a mop.

'Hello,' said Nanny Piggins. 'I'm Nanny Piggins.'

'I don't speak English,' said the cleaning woman in perfect English.

'What?' asked Nanny Piggins.

'I only speak Chinese,' said the cleaning woman.

'Really?' said Nanny Piggins. 'You don't look Chinese.'

'All right,' said the cleaning woman. 'I only speak Portuguese.'

'*Onde fica o grande gerente?*' asked Nanny Piggins (which is how you say 'Where is the big boss?' in Portuguese).

'I'm also a deaf mute,' said the cleaning woman.

'You don't have to feel threatened by me,' said Nanny Piggins. 'I've just been sent by my probation officer as part of my community service.'

'Oooh,' said the cleaning woman, 'so you're today's convict. Sorry, I thought you were from the health department. And I've been given strict instructions not to tell them where we buy our cleaning products.'

'Where do you buy your cleaning products?' asked Samantha.

'I can't tell you,' said the cleaning woman. 'Once you know you have to pretend you can only speak Chinese.'

'Who's in charge here?' asked Nanny Piggins.

'Some up-and-coming 29-year-old investment analyst from a big merchant bank in town,' said the cleaning woman.

'Where is he?' asked Nanny Piggins.

'Not here,' said the cleaning woman. 'He doesn't like the smell of old people. Besides, it's a different up-and-coming investment analyst every week. They keep getting promoted to a better job, or leaving to serve jail-time for insider trading.'

'But there must be some kind of manager here?' said Nanny Piggins.

'No,' said the cleaning woman. 'The manager had the highest salary, so she was first to go. The 29-year-old said it was a new decentralised management strategy.'

'What? So there's no-one in charge and no-one knows what they're doing?' asked Nanny Piggins.

'Exactly,' said the cleaning woman. 'Admittedly, it is very similar to the old centralised management strategy. The old manager used to drink a lot.'

The cleaning woman started mopping the floor again and Nanny Piggins, Boris and the children watched her edge away.

'What are you going to do?' asked Samantha.

'Well, I'm supposed to be keeping the old people company, and helping them come to terms with the loss of their television,' said Nanny Piggins. 'So I suppose I'd better find out where the old people are kept.'

Nanny Piggins, Boris and the children made their way down a long green hallway that opened out into a large common room.

'Finally!' exclaimed Nanny Piggins, upon sighting a dozen elderly people sitting around in plastic-covered armchairs. 'Some old people to do my community service on. Hello, I'm Nanny Piggins!'

The old people did not move or say a word. They just kept staring catatonically into the middle distance.

'Do you suppose they've eaten too much cake?' asked Nanny Piggins. 'I sometimes feel like that after 60 or 70 chocolate mud cakes.'

'Why don't I try to fix the TV?' suggested Boris.

'Good idea,' agreed Nanny Piggins.

'Hang on,' said Boris as he peered at the ancient TV set. 'Someone's broken off most of the knobs!'

Nanny Piggins had a closer look. 'They've broken the knobs off for all the good channels!'

'And look at this sign,' said Samantha.

On top of the TV set was a sign printed in bold block letters saying:

DO NOT, UNDER ANY CIRCUMSTANCES, SHOW THE OLD PEOPLE ANYTHING OTHER THAN BALLROOM DANCING OR LAWN BOWLS. IT ONLY GETS THEM OVER-EXCITED.

Nanny Piggins looked at her watch. '*The Young and the Irritable* is on in twenty minutes. Boris, run home and fetch our television.'

'But what if they get overexcited?' whispered Michael, looking worriedly at the catatonic old people.

'It would do them a world of good,' said Nanny Piggins. 'Now, while we're waiting for Boris, let's look about.'

Upstairs Nanny Piggins and the children found a long corridor with bedrooms on either side. 'I'm going to start introducing myself to more residents,' said Nanny Piggins, raising her trotter to knock on the first door. 'Hello, I'm Nanny Pigg–'

But as the door swung open Nanny Piggins was horrified to be confronted by a masked figure, wearing all black and holding a ticking bomb.

'Aaaaggghhh!' screamed Nanny Piggins and the children.

'Sorry,' said the figure, pulling off the ski-mask to reveal that she was really a sweet old lady. 'I'm Mrs Hastings and this isn't really a bomb. It's just a couple of empty shampoo bottles painted black, my alarm clock and some pretty coloured wires from out of the back of the television.'

'What on earth are you doing dressed like that and carrying a fake bomb?' asked Nanny Piggins.

'I was going to catch the 10.15 bus into town to rob the bank,' explained Mrs Hastings.

'Why were you going to rob a bank?' asked Nanny Piggins.

'Probably to buy a new television,' guessed Michael.

'No,' said Mrs Hastings. 'I'm not really going to rob a bank,' she chuckled. 'I'm going to let them catch me. Then they'll put me in jail. I'm hoping if I hit one of the policemen over the head with my handbag I'll get life imprisonment.'

'Why do you want to get life imprisonment?' asked Nanny Piggins.

'Because the food is much better in prison than it is here,' said Mrs Hastings. 'Plus you get an hour in the exercise yard every day. We're never allowed out in the yard here; the neighbours complain we're bad for local property prices.'

'That can't be right,' said Derrick. 'That food is better in prison than in a nursing home?'

'Oh it is,' said Mrs Hastings. 'Doris from room 4B was the first to think of it. She got herself put away for attempting to murder the visiting library lady. I went and visited her in prison and she says they get pesto every Tuesday, chicken cacciatore every Wednesday and once a month they have Mexican night with as many tacos as they can eat!'

'What are their desserts like?' asked Nanny Piggins, wondering for a millisecond if perhaps she had made a mistake in agreeing to community service if there was secretly a brilliant catering regimen at the local women's prison.

'It's mainly tinned fruit and custard,' admitted Mrs Hastings.

'Hmm,' said Nanny Piggins. She liked custard.

'But every Saturday, as a treat, they get carrot cake,' added Mrs Hastings.

'Carrot cake!' exclaimed Nanny Piggins. 'How dreadful! I didn't know they were allowed to torture people in jail. Offering them cake, then purposefully tainting it with vegetables. It makes me feel sick just thinking about it. Still, I suppose if you break the law you deserve to be punished.'

'You broke the law,' Michael reminded her.

'Yes,' agreed Nanny Piggins. 'And I suppose I should be thankful the judge didn't think to give me any carrot-cake-related punishment.'

Suddenly they were interrupted by a loud BOOM! The building shook and plaster fell from the ceiling.

'Now that *was* a bomb!' exclaimed Nanny Piggins.

'Yes, that's just the man in 12C,' explained Mrs Hastings. 'He's new. He isn't reconciled to being here yet.'

Nanny Piggins and the children went to investigate. Nanny Piggins nudged open the door of 12C, more cautiously this time, calling softly, 'Hello?' She didn't want to startle a geriatric armed with explosives.

But when the door swung open she was again shocked, this time on coming face-to-face with her old friend, the Retired Army Colonel from around the corner (who was deeply in love with her). He was sitting in a wheelchair with his two legs in plaster casts sticking straight out in front of him.

'Colonel!' exclaimed Nanny Piggins. 'What are you doing here? And why are you trying to blow everything up?'

'I'm not trying to blow everything up,' protested the Colonel. 'I'm just trying to fine-tune my propulsion system.'

'Propulsion system for what?' asked Nanny Piggins.

'My flying machine,' said the Retired Army Colonel, whipping back a sheet to reveal a homemade helicopter crafted out of canvas and sticks.

'That looks like something from the drawings of Leonardo da Vinci,' said Derrick in awe.

'It is based on the drawings of da Vinci,' admitted the Colonel. 'When I rang up the Air Force and asked for the specs on a Black Hawk helicopter they refused to give them to me. So I had to make do with this da Vinci postcard my niece sent me from the British Museum.' He showed them a dog-eared slip of card.

'But why do you need a helicopter?' asked Nanny Piggins.

'To escape, of course,' said the Colonel. 'When an officer is taken prisoner, his first duty is to attempt to escape.'

'But couldn't you just walk out the front door and catch a bus?' asked Nanny Piggins.

'I tried that,' said the Colonel, 'but I couldn't get down the stairs with my legs like this.'

Nanny Piggins looked at the large plaster casts encasing each of his legs. 'And how did you do that to yourself?'

The Retired Army Colonel blushed (which is something he usually only did after several glasses of the finest single malt whisky). 'Um, I'd rather not say. Trifle embarrassing, I'm afraid.'

Fortunately dear reader, I can tell you, as long as you promise not to tell Nanny Piggins. You see the Retired Army Colonel was so desperately in love with Nanny Piggins that he really wanted to impress her. In the past he had tried to catch her attention by arranging aeronautical acrobatic displays over her house and military brass bands to parade up and down her street. But these attempts had gone largely unnoticed. So the Colonel, being a brilliant strategic thinker, had decided to change tactics.

He decided to play Nanny Piggins at her own game. Having never cooked anything in his life, he now embarked on teaching himself how to bake a cake. Unfortunately, it had all gone horribly wrong when he turned his cake mixer up too high, and egg whites had flown out all over his kitchen, causing him to slip on the linoleum and fall down his back stairs, breaking both legs. (The whole incident had only given him an even greater admiration for Nanny Piggins because he knew she baked cakes every day, sometimes several times a day, and rarely broke any of her own limbs in the process.)

'But how did you get all the materials?' asked Nanny Piggins, looking around at the huge sheets of canvas, welding gear and C4 explosives.

'A dear lady and a true friend,' said the Colonel. 'Mrs Simpson.'

'Our Mrs Simpson?!' exclaimed Samantha.

'The one who lives next door?!' exclaimed Michael.

'And always gives us marshmallows, even if Nanny Piggins has been sending us over to raid her larder when she's lying down taking a nap?!' exclaimed Derrick.

'That's the one,' agreed the Colonel. 'Quite a lady.'

'But where did she get it all from?' marvelled Nanny Piggins.

'Well, she borrowed the canvas by cutting down one of the sails from a yacht at the harbour and she got the sticks from Mrs Lau's tomato patch,' explained the Colonel.

'What about the C4?' asked Nanny Piggins.

'I believe she plays bridge with a lady whose husband is very big in the mining industry, and they did a swap for Mrs Simpson's dolmades recipe,' explained the Colonel.

'Samantha, make a note to speak to Mrs Simpson next time we need high explosives,' said Nanny Piggins.

'But how did you end up in here?' asked Michael.

'The hospital arranged it,' explained the Colonel. 'I was hopped up on painkillers and couldn't fight them. Well, I tried fighting them, but the head nurse got cross when I put her in a headlock. Anyway, they said I couldn't go home on my own because there was no-one to look after me.'

'We would have looked after you!' protested Nanny Piggins.

'That's what I said,' agreed the Colonel, 'but they thought my stories of a glamorous accomplished flying pig swooping in to look after me were the product of my concussed mind, so they just upped my medication and dumped me here.'

'That's dreadful,' said Nanny Piggins.

'Not as dreadful as the food they serve here,' said the Colonel. 'You know I was a prisoner of war, and let me tell you the cockroaches I ate then were better and more nutritious than the meals we're served here.'

'Not for much longer,' said Nanny Piggins. 'I'm not having elderly people re-inventing da Vinci's flying machines, robbing banks and catatonically staring into space on my watch. I'm going to do something about it.'

'But Nanny Piggins, remember you're here to do community service,' said Samantha. 'You're not going to do something that gets you in even more trouble, are you?'

'Some things are worth risking your personal liberty for,' said Nanny Piggins. 'Freedom of speech, freedom to vote, and freedom to not eat really horrible food. In fact, if you've got good food you don't really need freedom of speech and voting rights. Which is why all sensible dictators hand out chocolate brownies if they want to maintain their evil regimes.'

As Nanny Piggins and the children made their way back downstairs they began to hear the rumble of noise.

'What's that?' asked Samantha worriedly.

'It sounds like people yelling,' said Nanny Piggins.

And as they entered the common room they discovered all the previously catatonic old people were now extremely animated. Some were waving Zimmer frames and some were trying to stand up so they could shake their fists. And they were all yelling at Boris who, characteristically enough, was fighting to hold back tears. (He did not like yelling, except when audiences yelled 'Bravo!', 'Encore!' and 'You are the best ballet dancing bear I've ever seen.' And even that made him cry.)

'What's got them so upset?' asked Derrick.

'Listen!' urged Nanny Piggins.

The children listened to what the old people were yelling.

'But who's Bethany's real mother?' cried an old lady wearing a crocheted hat.

'And how did Vincent kidnap Bridge and force him to become an international modelling superstar?' called an old man with two hearing aids.

'How can Brianna be Astra's baby when she clearly isn't African–American?' asked an old lady, who was starting to sob because she was so confused.

'Oh Sarah, I'm so glad you're here,' said Boris. 'They loved watching *The Young and the Irritable* but they've got so many questions and this man keeps hitting me with his oxygen stand. What am I going to do?'

'Turn the TV back on,' advised Nanny Piggins, 'and show them *The Bold and the Spiteful*. I'll go to the kitchen and get them some lunch.'

'Noooo!' screamed the old people suddenly and in unison.

'Please don't feed us any more of that horrible muck,' pleaded the old lady with the crocheted hat.

'We promise to be good,' said the man with two hearing aids.

'I won't hit the bear anymore,' promised the man who had used his oxygen stand as a weapon.

'Never fear,' said Nanny Piggins. 'I'm going to the kitchen to make sure you get a proper lunch.'

'What does that mean?' asked the crocheted-hat lady. 'Are you going to give us proper vegetables?'

'I can if you want,' said Nanny Piggins, 'but I was planning to start with a really nice cake.'

The old people cheered joyously as Nanny Piggins marched off in the direction of the kitchen.

When she got there Nanny Piggins found three apathetic middle-aged women, emptying processed frozen nuggets onto baking trays and stirring giant pots of grey–green goo that the packet said was reconstituted powdered peas.

The women took one look at Nanny Piggins' steely glare and realised the jig was up. They did not wait for her to start chasing them about with a cooking ladle before they tried to make a run for it. Luckily Nanny Piggins got in a good whack on each of their bottoms before they escaped out the back door, as she yelled angry warnings at them never to attempt to mass-poison old people with horrible, overcooked vegetables again.

'What are we going to do now?' asked Derrick. 'We've got half an hour to make lunch for 50 old people or they are going to start a riot.'

'And there's no real food here,' said Michael, peering into the cupboard. 'Unless you count generic tinned broccoli.'

'Which I certainly do not,' said Nanny Piggins, opening up her purse. 'Fortunately I had the foresight to borrow your father's credit card before I left the house this morning. Derrick, you're best at forging his signature – take it down to the supermarket and buy 20 bags of flour, 20 bags of sugar, 10 dozen eggs, 20 litres of cream and 200 chocolate bars.'

'That'll make a lot of cakes,' agreed Derrick, 'but what about a main course?'

'Cake will be the main course today,' declared Nanny Piggins. 'These retirees are clearly under-nourished and need building up.'

By the time Derrick got back with the ingredients there was only five minutes left in *The Bold and the Spiteful*.

'What are we going to do?' wailed Samantha. 'We can't make enough cake for 50 old people in five minutes.'

'You're right,' agreed Nanny Piggins. 'We're not going to.'

'You're going to let the old people starve?' asked Michael.

'Of course not,' said Nanny Piggins. 'I'm going to get them in here and make them do the cooking.'

'Can you do that?' asked Derrick.

'Forcing people to cook is the greatest gift you can give them,' said Nanny Piggins.

'I thought you said cake was the greatest gift you can give,' said Derrick.

'Yes, which is why forcing someone to make cake is such a kindness,' explained Nanny Piggins.

Just then they heard the closing theme music to *The Bold and the Spiteful* from the next room, then the sound of the old people starting to yell at Boris again.

'All right,' said Nanny Piggins. 'Get them in here and get their ingredients ready.'

It soon became apparent that Nanny Piggins' idea of setting the old people to work in the kitchen was even more brilliant than she could have imagined. Because the old people were so old they had all learnt to cook back in the days before anti-butter propaganda, when a woman could tip an entire litre of cream into a sauce without having to do nine hours of Pilates afterwards.

And it was not all cake. They soon discovered that Mr Lessandro had been secretly growing tomatoes on the fire escape. So after they had all had several helpings of dessert, he whipped up a delicious pasta dish with nothing more than tomatoes, basil, lemon juice and an entire bucket of cream.

Then Mrs Broomfield, who was normally so forgetful she could never recall her own cat's name, suddenly remembered a delicious recipe for jammy dodgers she had been taught as a girl. So they spent the rest of the afternoon happily working away in the kitchen, fine-tuning her shortbread and jam recipe.

Finally, as the sun began to set, Mrs Clemenceau mentioned that she had been a pastry chef during the war, so she was put in charge of organising dinner. And they ate a three-course meal of cheese soufflé for entree, chocolate soufflé for dessert and chocolate soufflé with extra chocolate for second dessert.

'That was the most delicious meal I have ever tasted,' announced Nanny Piggins as she wiped the last smear of chocolate soufflé from her snout.

'What about the chocolate meringue you made for dinner last night?' asked Michael.

'Mmm yes, that was good too,' agreed Nanny Piggins. 'But don't distract me, I'm having another brilliant idea. You old people should open a restaurant.'

'But we can't do that!' protested Mr Lessandro. 'We're old.'

'But there are 50 of you,' said Nanny Piggins, 'so you can share the work and take lots of naps.'

Just then the back door burst open and a weedy 29-year-old in a suit walked in.

'What's going on here?' he demanded.

The old people groaned.

'I knew he'd turn up and spoil our fun,' said Mrs Hastings. 'He's the 29-year-old investment banker who's in charge.'

'I've had complaints that staff have been assaulted with a cooking ladle,' complained the 29-year-old, 'and that old people have been seen climbing over the neighbourhood fences, stealing fruit.'

'We had to make jam somehow,' said Nanny Piggins. 'You're the one who wouldn't let the old people have a fruit and vegetable garden.'

'We have to maintain the look of the exterior of the building,' protested the 29-year-old, 'or the neighbours complain.'

'We've solved that problem. There won't be any more complaints,' Nanny Piggins assured him. 'We've been blasting the neighbours in the face with a hosepipe if they are rude enough to poke their noses over the fence.'

'Have you people been taking your medication?' demanded the 29-year-old, speaking to the old people as though they were three-year-olds.

'I've been medicating them myself,' announced Nanny Piggins, 'with proper food containing the five essential food groups – chocolate, cream, butter, sugar and cake.'

'I'm calling a doctor,' said the 29-year-old, taking out a mobile phone.

'Colonel, confiscate his phone,' ordered Nanny Piggins.

The Colonel loved following orders, especially from his favourite pig, so he soon had the 29-year-old in a painful wristlock, forcing him to drop the phone to the floor, where Mr Bernard crushed it with several lusty blows from his oxygen stand.

'What are you doing?' asked the 29-year-old.

'I'm taking over this old people's home and

turning it into a five-star gourmet restaurant,' announced Nanny Piggins.

The old people cheered.

'You can't do that,' protested the 29-year-old.

'Why not?' demanded Nanny Piggins.

'You can't start a restaurant without business models, cash flow assessments and market analysis,' babbled the 29-year-old.

'Pish!' said Nanny Piggins. 'Just you watch me.'

So Nanny Piggins set to work transforming the Golden Willows Retirement Home. She put Mrs Hastings in charge as restaurant manager, because any woman who could stage a bank robbery obviously had excellent planning skills. She made Mrs Clemenceau head chef, Mr Lessandro sous chef, and Mrs Broomfield chief chef in charge of jammy dodgers. Then Nanny Piggins forced the 29-year-old to become maître d'.

'But I'm an investment banker,' protested the 29-year-old. 'I can't spend the whole day away from the office.'

'It'll do you good,' said Nanny Piggins as she lifted the car keys from his pocket. 'The people you work for are obviously profoundly morally bankrupt if they invest in old people's homes as a moneymaking scheme. You're much better off here, away from their corrupting influence.'

'But I want to be corrupted,' protested the 29-year-old, 'so I can make a lot of money and retire at 40.'

'Trust me,' said Nanny Piggins. 'You'll be fat, bald and well on the way to a terminal heart condition by forty. You'll be much better off if you start living your life today.'

And by the end of the week the Golden Willows Restaurant had people lining up around the block, desperate to try their delicious food. It turns out that there was a huge market of young people eager to try forbidden ingredients they had only heard of – like butter and cream – as well as a huge market of old people who could still remember the magical taste of their grandmother's cooking.

Even the 29-year-old had a good time. He found he was much better at seating guests and fetching drinks than he was at insider trading.

And after dinner every night the old people put on a show. All the dinner guests were invited outside to watch the Colonel launch his flying machine and do a turn around the garden. Sometimes he made it all the way around and back to the window and sometimes he crashed into the next door neighbour's sycamore tree; either way it was always spectacular.

The only downside was, by the end of the week, Nanny Piggins had also made herself totally redundant. The Golden Willows Restaurant was a thriving independent business and she was back in a probation officer's office, having only completed sixty-seven hours of community service.

'Oh dear, Nanny Piggins,' said the probation officer. 'If you're going to whittle away your 5000-hour community service requirement you are going to have to resist the urge to transform every institution I send you to into a huge profit-generating organisation.'

'I'm sorry,' apologised Nanny Piggins. 'I just can't help myself. It comes from being so very good at everything.'

But the children were not at all sorry. They were happy to get their nanny back, at least for a short while, until the probation officer could find another suitable (or unsuitable) job for Nanny Piggins.

CHAPTER 4

Madame Piggins and the Psychic Gift

Nanny Piggins had never been so bored in her life. When she agreed to chaperone the children's school excursion as part of her community service, she had assumed they would be going somewhere interesting like a scorpion farm, or a hot air balloon race, or at the very least, a cake factory. But no, Headmaster Pimplestock had organised it, so they were traipsing around The National Transport Museum. To Nanny

Piggins' way of thinking, museums were boring at the best of times, but to have an entire museum that only featured different forms of transport was too boring to be true. If she had to look at another train or bus while the curator droned on and on about 'kilowatts' and 'torque', she was sure she would slip into a coma.

The worst part was that the museum was supposed to be about transport but there was not a single room devoted to the history of the flying pig! Her own life story would be a thousand times more interesting than Adrian Krinklestein's, the inventor of the cog, and he had a whole display.

On top of that, the children were being forced to fill out a ridiculous questionnaire written by Headmaster Pimplestock to prove that they had listened to every word the curator said. Which totally prevented them from ignoring the curator and nipping off to the coffee shop for a few slices of cheesecake with their nanny.

So Nanny Piggins was standing there, in a room full of antique Victorian water pumps, trying to keep herself awake by thinking up new recipes for chocolate ice-cream (perhaps more chocolate?), when something caught her eye. Through a doorway at the far end of the room she caught a glimpse of something red and shiny. Without thinking, her trotters were drawn towards it.

'Where are you going?' whispered Samantha as her nanny began to wander away.

'As far away from that dreadful curator as possible,' said Nanny Piggins.

'Then I'm coming too,' said Michael, dumping his questionnaire in a bin.

Derrick followed, reasoning he was the oldest so it would be irresponsible to let his little brother get in trouble all alone.

And Samantha chased after them because, much as she did not want to get in trouble, she did not like being the one left behind to answer the angry and difficult questions.

So Nanny Piggins and the children left the dreary Victorian water-pump room and entered a huge airy pavilion with a high glass ceiling, so they could see the sunshine and blue sky above. But that was not the best thing about the room. The best thing was that it was chock full of dozens and dozens of aeroplanes. There were modern jets, old propeller planes and funny looking water planes. Some hung from the ceiling, some stood up on pedestals and some were parked on the ground. But the brightest and shiniest of all was the one Nanny Piggins had spotted first. It was a bright red World War I triplane with German insignia, so it was much *much* more exciting than a Victorian water pump.

'What a pretty machine,' said Nanny Piggins. 'What is it?'

'It's a German fighter plane from the first World War,' explained Derrick. (He had been forced to study World War I only the previous term.)

'That's a plane?' exclaimed Nanny Piggins. 'I don't believe it. Where does everybody sit?'

'Well, the pilot sits there and the passenger sits there,' said Derrick, pointing to the two openings in the chassis.

'But where does the stewardess sit? And how does she get the drinks cart up and down?' asked Nanny Piggins, totally baffled.

'I don't think they had drinks carts on World War I fighter planes,' said Samantha.

'No drinks carts!' exclaimed a horrified Nanny Piggins. 'Next you'll be telling me they didn't serve an in-flight meal!'

'Well . . .' began Samantha.

'No in-flight meal!' gasped Nanny Piggins. 'No wonder they were at war. They must have been so unhappy.' Nanny Piggins leaned her trotter on the wing of the plane, then immediately recoiled.

'This isn't a real plane! It's a fake!' cried Nanny Piggins.

'It is?' said Michael, totally delighted. He enjoyed it when his nanny started denouncing people. And discovering a forgery was sure to lead to a lot of denouncing.

'Listen,' continued Nanny Piggins, rapping the wing of the plane again. 'It's hollow and I think it's made of *canvas*!'

'Maybe planes were made of canvas back in the old days,' suggested Samantha.

'Don't be ridiculous! What would happen if it rained?' said Nanny Piggins.

Samantha had the mental image of a plane all limp and floppy like a wet beach towel.

'No, someone must have stolen the real plane and replaced it with this canvas replica,' said Nanny Piggins. 'Well, there's only one way we can find out for sure.'

'Call the police and ask them to bring down a forensic team to carbon date the material?' suggested Derrick.

'No, turn it on and see if it flies,' declared Nanny Piggins.

'Oh no,' said Samantha, sitting down on the ground and taking out her lunch. Not so she could eat anything, but so she could use the brown paper bag to hyperventilate into.

'But that'll never work,' protested Derrick.

'Why not?' asked Nanny Piggins as she walked around the plane, kicking the chocks out from in front of the wheels. 'This is a museum, isn't it? They are supposed to have restored everything to perfect working condition.'

'But would there still be petrol in the engine?' asked Michael.

'I don't see why not,' said Nanny Piggins. 'When the Germans lost the war I expect they had a lot more important things to think about than whether or not they had siphoned all the petrol out of their planes. Anyway, we'll soon see.' Nanny Piggins hopped into the pilot's seat.

'Oh dear,' moaned Samantha as she ducked her head between her knees – partly to avoid fainting and partly so she would not have to see her beloved nanny come to harm.

'Oh look!' said Nanny Piggins delightedly. 'The German flying ace who last used this plane left his goggles under the seat. How thoughtful of him.'

Nanny Piggins put on the goggles and revved the engine.

'It can't be a fake, that engine sounds fine,' said Derrick.

'Oh, we won't know for sure until we take it up,' said Nanny Piggins.

'Up where?' asked Michael. Even he was beginning to worry, and generally he was the least inclined to worry of any boy you could care to meet.

'For a spin,' said Nanny Piggins with a joyous glint in her eye.

The children had seen that glint before. Nanny Piggins always got it before she threw herself into one of her death-defying stunts, such as being fired out of a cannon, doing a backflip off the clothes line or returning a library book two days late.

'Do you even know how to fly an aeroplane?' asked Derrick.

'I am the greatest flying pig in all the world,' Nanny Piggins reminded him.

'Yes, but the principles are rather different when you haven't been blasted out of a cannon,' argued Derrick.

'Pish!' said Nanny Piggins, and with that she opened the throttle, released the brake and the plane started to roll forward.

At this point the security guard from the museum started running towards them. (Now you might be wondering why he had not taken action sooner, such as when Nanny Piggins turned on the noisy diesel engine of their 95-year-old German tri-plane. But you have to understand that the security man was a little deaf and he had fallen asleep while lip-reading the curator's incredibly boring talk on Victorian water pumps taking place in the next room.) But an elderly man with a heart condition was never going to run down Nanny Piggins in an aeroplane.

She shot down the full length of the hall (which was perfectly safe because the museum was so boring there were no members of the public for her to crash into) and then, just as Samantha hid her face in her jumper because she did not want to see Nanny Piggins slam into a brick wall, the plane took off. And as it lifted up into the air, the tri-plane transformed from a rickety old thing banging along the ground, into an elegant flying machine soaring through the sky. Well, as much sky as there was inside the room. Luckily for Nanny Piggins it was a huge room so she could comfortably do loops around and around.

'Stop that pig!' screamed the curator as he ran into the pavilion.

'How?' asked the befuddled security guard.

'Do I have to do everything myself?' complained the curator, and with that he leapt into a World War I British bi-plane, turned on the engine and took off after Nanny Piggins.

Goodness knows what he thought he could do to get Nanny Piggins to come down. They might have left petrol in the engines but the restoration team did have the sense to remove the bullets from the machine guns. So all the curator could do was chase Nanny Piggins around and around, which she rather enjoyed. She did loop-the-loops and barrel rolls and weaved in between all the planes hanging from the ceiling to confuse him. Then Nanny Piggins flew towards the sun so the curator would lose sight of her, before reappearing behind him, blowing raspberries.

Down on the ground all the school children cheered. The most boring school excursion had turned into the world's most exciting school excursion in just a few short moments.

Nanny Piggins eventually landed voluntarily when the plane ran out of petrol and started to sputter. She glided to a perfect landing, yanking on the handbrake and rolling the tri-plane to a halt in exactly the same position she had found it.

Unfortunately the curator was not such an adept pilot. When he tried to land he came in too fast, skidded all the way along the floor (making a mess of the patina) and slamming into the refrigerated cake stand out the front of the cafeteria, totally ruining the New York cheesecake Nanny Piggins had her eye on for afternoon tea, which so horrified Nanny Piggins that she actually started to cry. Fortunately, licking bits of New York cheesecake off the sides of the smashed refrigerated cake stand soon cheered her up.

Many hours later, when Nanny Piggins and the children were finally allowed home, they were not in the highest of spirits. True, Nanny Piggins had not been taken away to jail, which was a good thing. (The museum had decided not to press charges because they did not want an inquiry into why two of their aeroplanes on public display had petrol in their engines.) But they had insisted that she pay for the damages, which seemed bitterly unfair given that she had not caused any herself. It was the curator who had smashed the expensive refrigerated cake stand. But Nanny Piggins did feel bad about ruining a contraption whose sole purpose was displaying cake in ideal conditions, so she agreed to these terms.

'Where are we going to get twenty-thousand dollars?' asked Derrick.

'We could ask father to lend it to us,' suggested Samantha, and they all burst out laughing at such a ridiculous suggestion.

'But seriously, children,' said Nanny Piggins. 'We do need a money-making scheme.'

'We could get jobs,' suggested Michael.

'Dear child,' said Nanny Piggins. 'Things are bad, but they're not that bad.'

'We could sell something,' suggested Derrick.

'Probably not wise,' said Nanny Piggins. 'I think your father is beginning to be suspicious. I sold his antique four-poster bed last week. And he has been muttering about his room not looking quite the way it did. No, what we need is a money-making scheme.'

The children scratched their heads and thought hard, but they did not know much about money-making schemes. Derrick had a vague idea that they had something to do with asking people to lend you money, then taking all that money and running away on holiday. (Which just goes to show Derrick actually knew everything you need to know about running a hedge fund.)

'Aha! I've got it!' declared Nanny Piggins, leaping up from the sofa. 'I am going to become a fortune teller.'

The children were not entirely convinced that becoming a fortune teller was an easy way to make twenty-thousand dollars. But Nanny Piggins seemed even more chipper than usual as she set up a miniature circus tent on the footpath outside the front of the house.

'Michael, run and fetch the "Nanny Wanted" sign from the garage,' said Nanny Piggins.

'You're not going to hire a new nanny, are you?' asked a horrified Michael.

'Of course not. I want to make my own sign,' explained Nanny Piggins.

As soon as Michael returned with the old weather-beaten placard, Nanny Piggins repainted it in exotic lettering:

Madame Piggins Fortune Teller
$5
Enter if you dare

She then put on her best silk dressing-gown, wrapped a purple scarf around her head, took the statuette of Santa out of a snow globe so it looked like a crystal ball, and then disappeared into the tent. The children stood outside, wondering what would happen next.

'Well, come on,' called Nanny Piggins. 'You've got to come in here too. You're my assistants.'

The children breathed a sigh of relief. They might not think fortune telling was a brilliant money-making scheme but they were pretty sure watching Nanny Piggins telling fortunes would be brilliantly entertaining. So they sat inside the tent, playing cards with Nanny Piggins and waiting for their first customer.

Seven hours later, Nanny Piggins did not seem at all perturbed that there had not been a single person enter the tent. 'It always takes a while to establish a small business,' she said wisely, as she won her one hundred and thirty-seventh game of snap in a row. They had almost forgotten why they were crouching on the floor of a miniature circus tent when a young woman entered.

'I was just on my way home when I saw your sign,' said the woman. 'You've got a front charging people five dollars to tell them a load of malarky.'

Nanny Piggins looked the woman up and down, sizing her up. 'As you are my first customer I am prepared to offer you a discount. I shall tell you three things from your future for the bargain price of $4.99.'

'All right,' said the woman, 'I could do with a

laugh, and my mum is not expecting me home for another half hour so I might as well.'

The young woman sat down and held out her palm for Nanny Piggins to read.

'Oh I don't read those,' said Nanny Piggins. 'I rub heads.'

'What?' exclaimed Derrick. He had not seen that one coming.

'If you want to know what is going on in someone's brain you can't tell by looking at their hand,' said Nanny Piggins, as though this was perfectly obvious. 'You've got to go right to the source and rub their head.' So Nanny Piggins leaned across the table, grabbing the woman's head between her trotters, and rubbed it. 'Hmmm, interesting,' muttered Nanny Piggins.

'What is it?' asked the woman scornfully. 'Does my dead granny want to tell me to wrap up warm this winter?'

'I'm a fortune teller, not a psychic. Do pay attention,' scolded Nanny Piggins as she continued to rub the woman's head. 'Okay, I can see it clearly. You are going to . . .' Nanny Piggins paused here for dramatic effect.

'Yes?' said the young woman, who could not help but be curious.

'Lose a button from your cardigan,' said Nanny Piggins, 'and . . . bang your head on a frozen fish. And . . . meet a man who is always wet.'

Nanny Piggins then let go of the woman's head and sat back with an air of triumph about her.

'What?' said the young woman.

'I have made my predictions for your future,' said Nanny Piggins with finality.

'You've talked a load of old hogwash,' said the woman.

'That will be $4.99 please,' said Nanny Piggins, holding out her trotter.

'If you think I'm going to pay for that utter –' began the young woman.

'Oh dear,' said Nanny Piggins, suddenly with an edge of menace in her voice. 'Michael, I think you had better fetch Boris.'

'Who's Boris?' asked the young woman.

'The giant bear who lives in our garden,' said Samantha truthfully.

'I predict he is about to get very angry,' said Nanny Piggins.

The young woman decided to cut her losses. She handed over the money and left in a sulk, muttering about con artists and how she had a good mind to call the police.

'That didn't go well,' said Derrick.

'We'll see,' said Nanny Piggins smugly, whistling to herself as she packed up her fortune-telling paraphernalia. 'I think that will do for today.'

'But you've only told one fortune,' protested Michael.

'And you only charged $4.99,' said Samantha, 'so you've got another $19,995.01 to earn.'

'All in good time,' said Nanny Piggins. 'Come along. Since you have been such good children I'll make chocolate fondue for dinner.'

'It's Tuesday, you always make chocolate fondue on Tuesdays,' said Michael.

'Yes, I'm lucky that you always behave so well on Tuesdays,' said Nanny Piggins.

The next day Nanny Piggins kept the children home from school. She rang Headmaster Pimplestock and told him they had all simultaneously contracted lead poisoning from too much sucking on pencils. Then she hung up and took the phone off the hook before he had a chance to consult a medical dictionary. Next they went outside and began re-erecting the tent. They had only just got the tent pegs banged into the root stocks of Mr Green's pedigree rose plants when the young woman from the previous day burst back into the tent.

'Good morning,' said Nanny Piggins brightly, as though this sudden arrival was entirely to be expected.

'You're a genius!' gushed the young woman.

'Yes,' agreed Nanny Piggins.

'A savant . . . a wonder . . . an inexplicable force of nature,' gabbled the woman.

'All true,' concurred Nanny Piggins.

'You mean to say that Nanny Piggins' predictions actually happened?' asked Michael, being the first of the children to grasp the woman's strange ramblings.

'See for yourself,' said the woman, holding up her cardigan.

'See what?' asked Derrick.

'Exactly,' said the young woman. 'There's nothing there. The button is missing!'

All three children gasped in amazement.

'But what about being hit in the head with a frozen fish?' asked Samantha.

'Well, I went to a sushi restaurant last night, and as the chef was walking through the restaurant with a great big frozen tuna on his shoulder, someone called out to him, and when he turned around to say hello, the tuna's tail whacked me in the head. Look!' said the young woman, holding up her fringe and showing them a big black bruise right in the middle of her forehead.

'Amazing!' said Samantha. 'But surely you didn't meet a man who is always wet?'

'I went to the sushi restaurant on a blind date with a man who is a marine biologist. He goes scuba diving every day,' said the young woman.

'So he's always wet!' gasped Samantha.

'Exactly,' said the young woman. 'Every word you said came true.'

'I know,' said Nanny Piggins. 'I don't do things I'm bad at.'

'Can you do it again? Because I've brought along some friends who want to have their fortunes read too,' said the young woman.

'Of course,' said Nanny Piggins. 'Send the first one in.'

And so Nanny Piggins' fortune-telling business took off. Word spread quickly. By the end of the week there were queues wrapped around the block from five o'clock in the morning onwards. And, amazingly, every single prediction Nanny Piggins made came true.

She told the butcher he would accidentally cut off a pinkie finger. And the next day he did. Luckily for him it was not his own – it was the work experience boy's, and he was not disappointed. The doctors sewed it back on and he had quite the story to boast about when he went back to school on Monday.

She told a young lonely man with a secret passion for flamenco dancing that he would meet the woman of his dreams if he went outside the tent and found the seventeenth person in the queue. And indeed there was a lonely young woman with a secret desire to wear a frilly gypsy dress and rhythmically stamp her feet, standing right there.

She told Hans the Baker that he would find his television remote control if he looked in his freezer. And it was true. (His wife, Princess Annabelle, had put it there to punish him for leaving a very dirty ring around the bathtub. Now you have to understand, Hans and Annabelle had a very loving, happy marriage. And she was a broad-minded princess who did not mind a bit of dirt. But in this instance the dirt was in fact a caramel stain, where Hans had secretly been eating the leftover caramel éclairs from the shop without her. This was a sin that could not go unpunished.)

And she told Headmaster Pimplestock he would

have a very boring life punctuated only by encounters with a glamorous and beautiful pig (which, admittedly, any one of the children could have predicted).

In just five days she had raked in $20,001.09.

'Look at all this lovely money,' said Nanny Piggins, heroically resisting the urge to roll in it.

'Now you can repay the museum,' said Samantha happily. She hated trouble in all its forms. It weighed heavily on her that Nanny Piggins was banned for life from the Transport Museum, even though Nanny Piggins was not bothered at all. (She actually cheered and threw her hat in the air when she found out.)

'Yes, I suppose I have to,' conceded Nanny Piggins reluctantly. The curator at the Transport Museum seemed particularly unworthy of large amounts of cash money. But when she thought of the poor broken cake stand, Nanny Piggins got a lump in her throat. 'We'll take it straight there this afternoon. But the fortune-telling business is going so well. There's nothing to stop us making our own $20,000 next week.'

'I suppose not,' admitted Samantha. 'It would be nice to have such a large amount of pocket money.'

'You could even tell fortunes for two weeks and make $40,000,' said Derrick.

'Or three weeks and earn $60,000,' said Michael.

'What a good idea,' said Nanny Piggins. 'We could have a lot of fun with $60,000. We could travel the world trying exotic foreign cakes and learning new and exciting ice-cream recipes.'

'And build a monster robot that crushes cars,' said Michael.

'Oh yes, obviously that too,' agreed Nanny Piggins.

But their planning session was, at that very moment, interrupted when the lights in the tent flickered on and off, smoke billowed in under the entry flap, strange eastern music filled the air and a doorbell rang.

'What's going on?' asked Derrick.

'And why is there smoke in here?' asked Samantha.

'And who installed a doorbell in the tent?' asked Michael.

'Oh dear,' said Nanny Piggins. 'I know of only one woman who uses such elaborate special effects before making her entrance. I think I am in trouble.'

'Not again,' sighed Samantha.

'Derrick, you had better open the front flap

of the tent, and if you find a beautiful and exotic African sorceress there, do let her in,' said Nanny Piggins as she picked up a plate of chocolate, ready to welcome her guest. 'Children, prepare yourselves. You are about to meet a real fortune teller, the one from the circus.'

A moment later a beautiful and exotic sorceress glided into the tent. (Nanny Piggins' predicting ability extended to knowing who was at the door.)

'Hello Madame Zandra, so good to see you,' said Nanny Piggins politely.

'Sarah Piggins,' boomed Madame Zandra in her beautiful resonant voice. 'You should be ashamed of yourself.'

'Oh, I am,' Nanny Piggins assured her.

'Those with the gift of fortune telling have a responsibility to uphold the rules of mystical power,' said Madame Zandra sternly. 'When I taught you my secrets you promised to abide by these rules.'

'Sorry, I forgot. I must have had too little chocolate that day. The rules slipped my mind,' confessed Nanny Piggins.

'Then I shall remind you of them. Rule One: a fortune teller must always muddle her predictions up with gobbledegook and bunkum,' intoned Madame Zandra.

'Of course,' said Nanny Piggins.

'If you tell fortunes accurately you're going to put the rest of us out of business,' said Madame Zandra. 'Do you really want a whole crowd of angry unemployed fortune tellers on your doorstep?'

'No, Madame Zandra,' said Nanny Piggins humbly.

'And Rule Two: always keep your tent properly ventilated,' coughed Madame Zandra as she flapped her hand in front of her face, 'so you can use lots of smoke in your special effects.'

'You're so right, Madame Zandra, I don't know what I was thinking,' agreed Nanny Piggins. 'However, I predict that you won't punish me too severely, because you're so lovely and you would quite fancy some of the treacle tart I have hidden in my turban.'

And so Nanny Piggins closed her fortune-telling business. On the whole she was glad to do it. While having $60,000 would be nice, having jobs was not. So it was much better to have just one instead of two. Madame Zandra left after making Nanny Piggins swear never to tell an accurate fortune again. Then Nanny Piggins and the children went down to the Transport Museum to pay for their damages.

When they got to the museum, however, the most remarkable thing happened. For a start they could not get into the building, and not just because Nanny Piggins was banned but because there was police tape across the front entrance. Naturally, Nanny Piggins just ducked under the tape and went inside. Then, after several police constables tried (and failed) to crash-tackle her in the lobby, the Police Sergeant intervened and told her that she did not need to repay the museum.

It turns out Nanny Piggins had been entirely right. The World War I fighter planes were fakes. The curator had sold the real planes over the internet and substituted them with forgeries he had made in his own garage. (Which is why they had petrol in their engines, because he had flown them in to work early one morning before anybody else got in.) So the curator was being forced to pay for all the damages himself.

This meant Nanny Piggins, Boris and the children returned home with the $20,000 still in their possession. The cash sat on the coffee table while they stared at it.

'It's such a lot of money,' said Samantha reverentially.

'What are we going to spend it on?' asked Derrick.

'A honey farm?' suggested Boris.

'A medium-sized monster robot?' suggested Michael.

'No,' said Nanny Piggins. 'While they are excellent suggestions, I have an even better idea.'

Later that day Nanny Piggins, Boris and the children went out and bought their very own refrigerated cake stand. They put it right in the middle of the kitchen. Nanny Piggins was so proud of their purchase she actually polished it (and as you know she did not normally believe in housework). Of course, the cake stand remained empty at all times. You see, it did its job too well. Whenever Nanny Piggins put a cake in there it looked so good, how could she resist eating it? But she enjoyed knowing she could store a cake if she chose to.

CHAPTER 5

Nanny Piggins and the Bump on the Head

'Nanny Piggins! Where are you?' shouted Derrick, as he, Samantha and Michael rushed upstairs to their nanny's room. Boris followed close behind.

Normally when they woke up in the morning, they went downstairs and found their nanny in the kitchen, making some wonderful sugar-filled delight. But occasionally, when Nanny Piggins was feeling lazy, she would get up an hour earlier, whip up a spectacular seven-course breakfast, then take it all back upstairs to her bedroom so they could enjoy breakfast in bed. Her room was all set up for it. Nanny Piggins had a camping stove in her dressing table for the omelette bar and a warming plate on her night stand to keep the pancakes at the perfect temperature. If anything else needed warming up she would just give it a good squeeze with her curling tongs. (She had an extra pair of curling tongs specifically for heating food.)

But on this morning, when the children burst into her room, they did not find Nanny Piggins surrounded by food, just putting the finishing touches on a profiterole tower. Instead she was lying in the middle of her bed, staring at the ceiling.

'What's wrong, Nanny Piggins?' asked Derrick.

'Are you sick?' worried Samantha.

'Has someone broken into your bedroom and superglued you to your bed?' asked Michael.

'No, I can move and I'm not sick,' said Nanny Piggins. 'But something is wrong.'

'You can't decide what to wear?' guessed Boris.

'Worse than that,' said Nanny Piggins.

Boris gasped. 'What could possibly be worse than not knowing what to wear?' (This just goes to show what an empathetic bear Boris was, because he did not even wear clothes himself.)

'I can't think what to do,' explained Nanny Piggins. 'Normally when I wake up in the morning my mind is bubbling with ideas for adventures and fun. But this morning when I opened my eyes, all I could think was: nothing.'

'How can you think nothing?' asked Derrick.

'I don't know,' admitted Nanny Piggins. 'But I am forever doing extraordinary things I did not know I was capable of. And thinking of nothing must just be another one.'

'Perhaps if you ate some cake,' suggested Samantha.

'I tried that,' said Nanny Piggins, pointing towards the dozens of Swiss roll packets strewn across the floor. 'And while that certainly made me feel better about thinking of nothing, it didn't help me think of something.'

'Do you want us to take you to the doctor?' asked Michael.

'Pish to that!' said Nanny Piggins. 'A doctor is hardly the person you turn to for original ideas. They wouldn't know how to tie their shoelaces if they hadn't been taught it at medical school. Which, incidentally, is why so many doctors wear loafers.'

'Then what are we going to do?' asked Derrick.

'Do you want us to stay home so we can look after you?' asked Samantha.

'Obviously you should all stay home from school,' agreed Nanny Piggins. 'But not so you can look after me. So you can help me, because I've had an idea about how to come up with an idea.'

'You have?' asked Derrick suspiciously.

'It's not going to be dangerous, is it?' asked Samantha.

'Of course not,' said Nanny Piggins. 'Well, not very.'

Five minutes later Nanny Piggins was standing in the backyard (still wearing her pyjamas) while Boris and the children hung out of the second storey window directly above, with a great big bucket of apples. (They did not have any apples in the house but Mrs Simpson next door did have several apple trees, so Nanny Piggins thought it would be an act of kindness if they were to pick them for her. Nanny Piggins assumed Mrs Simpson shared her belief that fruit and vegetables were an eyesore in any garden.)

'I think this is a terrible idea,' worried Samantha.

'Nonsense,' scoffed Nanny Piggins. 'If having an apple drop on his head gave Isaac Newton the idea of gravity, just think what it will do for me.'

'What exactly is gravity?' asked Michael.

'It's the reason –' sobbed Boris, breaking down into tears, 'we weigh so much when we stand on the bathroom scales.'

'There, there,' comforted Samantha. 'I'm sure the scales are wrong. They are probably broken.'

'They were definitely broken after Boris stood on them,' said Derrick under his breath.

'I'm sure being hit by an apple will help me come up with something much more interesting than one of the fundamental laws of physics,' said Nanny Piggins confidently. 'At the very least, a new apple strudel recipe.'

'But won't it hurt?' asked Samantha, holding a Granny Smith in her hand and thinking that the last thing in the world she wanted to do was to drop it on her nanny's head.

'That's the wonderful thing about head injuries,' said Nanny Piggins. 'If they are severe enough, you don't feel very much of anything at all. Besides, you forget that I am a former flying pig, and I was blasted out of a cannon hundreds of times before it occurred to me that perhaps I should be wearing a helmet. So I have an unusually thick skull.'

'Plus it is super strong because of all the calcium Sarah gets in her diet from eating so much butter and cream,' explained Boris.

'And chocolate!' added Nanny Piggins. 'Never forget that chocolate is a dairy food. Thanks to my high chocolate diet, you could drop anything you liked on my head and I'd be fine. Just don't drop any vegetables on me – it takes forever to get the smell out.'

'What type of apple would you like us to drop first?' asked Michael. 'A red gala or a Golden Delicious?'

'Surprise me,' said Nanny Piggins.

And so Michael dropped a Golden Delicious apple onto his nanny's head. His aim wasn't terribly good, so Nanny Piggins had to do some fancy footwork to make sure it hit her, but in the end it bopped her right on the top of her skull.

'Anything?' asked Boris.

'I did just remember where I put my house keys, but no brilliant plans for a day of exciting fun,' said Nanny Piggins sadly.

'How about I drop a Granny Smith on you?' suggested Derrick. 'They're bigger.'

'Good thinking,' enthused Nanny Piggins.

Unfortunately all the blow from the Granny Smith did was remind Nanny Piggins that she needed to buy nutmeg from the supermarket. Some time later, after 138 apples of varying varieties had been dropped on Nanny Piggins, she still had not come up with any brilliant ideas. She had not even come up with any revolutionary breakthroughs in physics – although she did remember that she'd put her romance novel in the freezer so that burglars would not steal it, that Tuesday was Mrs McGill's birthday, that Michael needed a haircut, that Addis Ababa was the capital of Abyssinia and that electric blue would be the perfect colour to repaint the downstairs bathroom.

'I don't understand it,' said Nanny Piggins. 'This having an apple dropped on my head isn't working for me at all. Perhaps I need to do what Benjamin Franklin did and fly a kite in an electrical storm.'

'No!' exclaimed all the children at once. It was one thing to drop fruit on their nanny's head, but they did not want to stand by and watch her get struck by lightning.

'You're probably right,' agreed Nanny Piggins. 'I'd hate to ruin our kite.'

'I've got an idea!' exclaimed Boris.

'How? Did an apple hit you?' asked Nanny Piggins.

'No, I came up with it on my own, just using my brain regularly,' said Boris.

'Good for you!' encouraged Nanny Piggins. 'What is it?'

'Wait here!' said Boris excitedly.

They all waited as they listened to Boris run out of the room, along the corridor, down the stairs, into the kitchen, open and shut several cupboards, then run back up the stairs and back into the bedroom. (Even though Boris was a ballet dancer and therefore very dainty, he was still a 700-kilogram bear, and sometimes when he was excited he would sound like one.)

Boris emerged at the window with a triumphant smile on his face, holding a watermelon. 'If the apples don't work, why don't we try a watermelon?' suggested Boris, proud of his idea.

'You can't drop a watermelon on Nanny Piggins' head!' squealed Samantha.

'Why not?' asked Boris. 'I'm sure it will still be good to eat afterwards.'

'But that watermelon is huge!' exclaimed Derrick.

'It's bigger than Nanny Piggins!' added Michael.

'You'll hurt her,' added Samantha.

'Piffle!' called Nanny Piggins. 'Just drop the thing. I'll be fine.'

'I won't let you!' said Michael, grabbing hold of Boris' arm. Samantha and Derrick grabbed at Boris too.

Now as you know, Boris was a *very* big bear, and three normal-sized children should have been no match for him. But he was also delicate of heart, so being roughly accosted by three of his four favourite people in the world shocked him deeply, and predictably made him cry. In his hurry to find a handkerchief so he could blow his nose, Boris dropped the watermelon without thinking. And when Nanny Piggins saw the watermelon coming she purposefully stepped into its path.

As soon as they heard the 'thud', the children and Boris instantly stopped their wrestling so they could look out the window. On the ground below they saw Nanny Piggins lying prostrate and surrounded by shattered chunks of watermelon.

'She looks so peaceful lying there,' said Derrick.

'And the watermelon goes beautifully with her sienna yellow pyjamas,' said Michael.

'Oh my goodness!' exclaimed Samantha. 'We've killed her.'

Boris just wailed.

(Now reader, please don't panic. As you can see, this is only Chapter 5 and there are another five chapters to come of this book, and my publisher would never let me kill the title character halfway through. So rest assured **Nanny Piggins is not dead**. It's just for purposes of dramatic storytelling – the children do not know that at this time.)

They all rushed downstairs to the garden. (Boris tried jumping directly out the window but he would not fit through.) When they reached their nanny she was breathing normally and there were no outward signs of head wounds.

'Nanny Piggins! Are you all right?' asked Derrick as they all knelt around her.

'Should we slap her?' asked Michael.

'You can,' said Derrick, 'but even if she's in a coma she'll probably still bite you.'

'Look, there's no need,' said Samantha. 'She's coming round.'

Nanny Piggins' eyes began to flutter open and she struggled to sit up.

'Are you all right?' asked Samantha. 'Do you want us to call an ambulance?'

'Ayyymmmmsooooso-o-orrrrrrreeee,' wailed Boris, crying with the shuddering intensity only a Russian can muster.

Nanny Piggins rubbed her head. 'What happened?' she asked.

'A watermelon slipped out of Boris' hands and fell onto your head,' explained Michael.

Boris wailed harder.

'A watermelon?' said Nanny Piggins, dazedly looking about at the shattered fruit surrounding her, and pulling a chunk from her hair.

'Would you like some medicinal chocolate?' asked Derrick.

'No, thank you,' said Nanny Piggins.

The children and Boris gasped. Now they were really worried about her.

'You don't want chocolate?!' asked Samantha.

'No, I want to know where I am,' said Nanny Piggins.

'In the garden,' said Michael.

'Who are you?' she asked, looking at the children, 'and who am I?' she added, rubbing her head.

'Oh no,' sobbed Boris. 'I hit her so hard, she's started asking profound philosophical questions. Next she'll be asking if a tree falling in the forest will make people clap!'

'No, it's worse than that!' exclaimed Derrick. 'Nanny Piggins has got amnesia!'

'Aaaaaaaggghhhhh!!!!' screamed Nanny Piggins as she suddenly leapt to her feet. 'There's a bear!'

'Of course, it's your brother, Boris,' explained Samantha.

'But how can a woman have a brother who's a bear?' asked Nanny Piggins.

The children looked at each other.

'Um, I'm not sure how to put this delicately,' said Derrick, 'but you're not a woman, you're a pig.'

'Don't be ridiculous!' said Nanny Piggins. 'How can I be a pig when I'm wearing such elegant pyjamas?'

'Aaaaaaggggggggghhhhh!!!' screamed Nanny Piggins, two minutes later when she saw her reflection in a mirror. 'I *am* a pig!'

'But a very, very beautiful one,' Michael assured her.

'I don't understand,' said Nanny Piggins. 'If I'm a pig and I'm not wearing a wedding ring, how did I come to have three children?' She turned to look at Derrick, Samantha and Michael.

'We're not your children,' explained Samantha.

'I'm a pig *and* a kidnapper!?' exclaimed a horrified Nanny Piggins.

'No, you're our nanny,' explained Michael.

Nanny Piggins slumped down in a chair. 'I'm a domestic servant? Why, that's even worse. At least if

I was a kidnapper I would be showing some career initiative.'

'I think we should take Nanny Piggins to see a doctor,' said Derrick. 'Aside from having no memories of anything, she doesn't seem to be thinking straight.'

After several X-rays, a CAT scan (which sadly did not involve an actual cat) and lots of prodding Nanny Piggins' head exactly where it hurt, the doctor took Boris and the children aside to tell them his conclusions.

'Your nanny is very lucky,' said the doctor. 'She has an unusually thick skull.'

'Yes, it's because chocolate is a dairy food,' explained Michael.

'But what about Nanny Piggins' amnesia?' asked Derrick. 'When will it go away?'

'It's hard to say. These things differ from case to case,' said the doctor.

'But I want my sister back,' sobbed Boris, while shaking the doctor by his lapels.

'I'm sorry,' said the doctor. 'The brain is a tricky thing.'

'You're a neurosurgeon and that's the best you can come up with?' scoffed Nanny Piggins. (She could hear every word he was saying because the curtain they were standing behind was not sound-proof.) 'Where did you get your medical degree? The back of a cereal packet?'

'I've got an idea!' exclaimed Boris, letting go of the doctor and whipping out a watermelon. 'How about I hit her over the head again?'

'No!' screamed everyone in the room.

'You have to give her brain time to heal,' explained the doctor. 'She will be all right. The human body has wonderful self-healing abilities.'

'She isn't a human, she's a pig,' Michael whispered to the doctor.

'Sorry, I keep forgetting,' admitted the doctor. 'She's just so attractive.'

Boris and the children took Nanny Piggins home and let her re-acquaint herself with the house while they tried to figure out what to do.

'Your father must be quite a man to have such a lovely house,' said Nanny Piggins as she looked around. 'Are he and I romantically involved?'

'Gross!' exclaimed all three children simultaneously.

'I only ask because I do remember from reading romance novels that nannies are catnip to men,' explained Nanny Piggins.

'What are we going to do with her?' asked Derrick.

'We can't go to school and leave her like this,' said Samantha.

'We'll just have to take the day off,' said Michael.

'If Nanny Piggins wasn't out of her mind, it's what she would want,' agreed Derrick.

Unfortunately no sooner had the children decided to play truant than Miss Britches, the truancy officer (and another one of Nanny Piggins' arch-nemeses) turned up. It was almost as if she had listening devices planted in the house and knew that their nanny had fallen ill. And without their nanny's superior shin-biting-, door-slamming-, and escape-route-finding skills, the children were defenceless. In fact, in her memory loss state Nanny Piggins invited the truancy officer in for a cup of tea and a chat, which the truancy officer took to be a ruse to slip her doctored cake, and so she grabbed the children and fled as fast as she could.

The children worried about their nanny all day. They found it even harder to concentrate on the tedious lessons and teacher waffle than usual. After a long day of learning nothing, they could not wait to get back to the house to see if their nanny was all right.

But when they burst into the living room, they were met with a horrible sight. There, in the best armchair, sat Nanny Piggins' arch nemesis – Nanny Anne. A nanny so perfectly perfect her hair looked like it had been ironed (as indeed it had, but Nanny Anne never admitted this because she did not want people to know that she did something as undignified as resting her head on an ironing board). They were shocked to see her because Nanny Piggins had banned Nanny Anne from entering their house ever since the time she had whipped an electric razor out of her handbag and tried to shave Michael's head, claiming to have seen a nit. He actually did have nits but Nanny Piggins' secret shampoo recipe (which primarily contained chocolate) remedied that in a way that was much kinder to the nits and Michael's hairstyle.

But even more horrifyingly, sitting right next to Nanny Anne was a woman who looked exactly like Nanny Anne in all respects, except for the fact that she was two feet shorter.

'Where's Nanny Piggins?' demanded Derrick.

Nanny Anne ignored them and turned to address her clone. 'Now this is exactly what I was just talking about,' smiled Nanny Anne. 'Your children need a lesson in manners. It isn't nice to burst in and start yelling at a guest.'

'You're no guest,' scoffed Samantha. 'Where's our nanny?'

'Sitting right in front of you,' said Nanny Anne with a smirk.

'Good afternoon children, did you have a good day at school?' asked the Nanny Anne clone.

The children recoiled in horror, for they now realised this clone was a pig. A pig who, if you ignored the bleached blonde hair, perky lavender twin-set and natty little pearl necklace, looked a lot like Nanny Piggins.

'It's one of Nanny Piggins' evil twin sisters!' exclaimed Michael.

'Who are you? Anthea, Beatrice, Abigail, Gretel, Deidre, Jeanette, Ursula, Nadia, Sophia, Sue, Charlotte, Wendy or Katerina? And what are you doing here?' demanded Derrick.

Nanny Anne laughed. 'Don't you recognise your own nanny when you see her?'

The children peered at the alien-looking pig.

'It can't be Nanny Piggins,' said Samantha. 'She would rather die than wear pearls. She takes the expression "pearls before swine" very personally.'

'And she'd never bleach her hair,' added Derrick. 'She likes referring to herself as a raven-haired beauty too much.'

'It is Nanny Piggins,' gasped Michael. 'Look, you can see the scar on her leg where she climbed up on the kitchen bench and banged into the toaster oven while she was trying to eat the pancake that was stuck to the ceiling.'

'What have you done to her?' accused Samantha.

'Nanny Anne has been kind enough to help me with my appearance,' said Nanny Piggins. 'There's so much I don't remember. And she has been telling me all the things I need to know about manners, politeness and being nice.'

'But you hate being nice,' argued Derrick. 'You prefer being fabulous or very cross or staggeringly beautiful.'

'You're never something as dull as *nice*,' said Michael.

'But Nanny Anne has been teaching me that as a nanny, it is my place to be dull,' said Nanny Piggins.

Nanny Anne nodded and smiled (a smile that looked nice but which the children knew to be pure wickedness).

'And Nanny Anne says that if I give her all my cake recipes she will let me join her etiquette club so I can socialise with the other nannies,' continued Nanny Piggins.

'But you hate etiquette,' protested Samantha.

'And you hate clubs,' added Michael.

'And you hate Nanny Anne,' added Derrick. 'Every time you turn your back she tries to wash behind your ears with a scouring pad.'

'Older boy, you must not say that,' said Nanny Piggins. 'Telling a guest that you hate them is bad etiquette.' Nanny Piggins looked to Nanny Anne for confirmation.

Nanny Anne nodded. 'And how are you going to punish him?' prompted Nanny Anne.

'I have to punish him?' asked Nanny Piggins, rubbing her head.

'Oh yes, punishment is character building,' said Nanny Anne. 'An outburst like that warrants, at the very least, being sent to bed without any supper.'

'But Nanny Piggins, you don't approve of withholding meals. You always say that the only people who should be sent to bed without any supper are murderers, to teach them a lesson, and people who don't eat chocolate, so they will come to their senses,' argued Samantha.

'Oh dear,' said Nanny Anne. 'Arguing in front of a guest is also bad etiquette.'

'It is?' asked Nanny Piggins.

'Oh yes,' said Nanny Anne. 'I think that requires some time in the naughty corner.'

'But Nanny Piggins usually encourages us to be naughty in all corners of the house,' countered Samantha.

'Tsk tsk tsk,' said Nanny Anne. 'Answering back, you can't accept that, Nanny Piggins.'

'I can't?' asked Nanny Piggins, her head starting to throb. 'All right, girl-child, you don't get any supper either.'

'I've had enough of this,' said Michael. 'I'm getting Boris and telling him to bring the water-melon.' Michael ran out of the room.

'Threatening to hit your nanny over the head with a watermelon is punishable too,' called out Nanny Anne.

'So the little boy doesn't eat either?' asked Nanny Piggins.

'That's right,' said Nanny Anne.

'I never realised that nannying was so like policing,' said Nanny Piggins.

'Oh it is a lot harder,' said Nanny Anne, 'because we aren't supposed to use batons and handcuffs.'

'What do I do now?' asked Nanny Piggins, as she looked at Samantha fuming in the newly established naughty corner and Derrick glaring at her from the couch.

'After a hard day nannying, I think we deserve a treat,' smiled Nanny Anne. 'I brought over a cake especially for you.'

'Really? What type of cake is it?' asked Nanny Piggins as Nanny Anne retrieved a plate of cake from her basket.

'Chocolate cake,' said Nanny Anne.

'That sounds nice,' said Nanny Piggins, perking up. She scooped up a polite little morsel of cake and put it in her mouth.

'With zucchini grated into it for extra fibre,' added Nanny Anne.

Nanny Piggins did not swallow. She held the cake in her mouth for a moment before her face began to turn a very disturbing shade of purple. Then Nanny Piggins' whole body began to shudder.

'Are you all right, Nanny Piggins?' asked Samantha.

Nanny Piggins did not speak. She was too busy pulling the most pained face the children had ever seen. Eventually when she could not stand it anymore, Nanny Piggins leapt to her feet and spat the glob of cake onto Mr Green's expensive Persian carpet.

'Phah, phah, phah!' said Nanny Piggins as she spat many more times, trying to get the taste out of her mouth, 'Are you trying to poison me?' She turned on Nanny Anne. 'Are you trying to murder me with vegetable-tainted cake?'

'Nanny Piggins, get a grip of yourself,' said Nanny Anne. 'You are being rude.'

'You are the one who is being rude!' denounced Nanny Piggins. 'Rude to the institution of cake by daring to bring a zucchini within a five-mile radius of one. How dare you! Samantha, fetch me the telephone. I am reporting Nanny Anne to the police for crimes against cake.'

'I think Nanny Piggins is feeling better,' said Derrick happily.

'There's no such thing as crimes against cake,' protested Nanny Anne.

'Then I shall run for parliament and have the laws introduced immediately,' declared Nanny Piggins. 'And I am keeping this cake –' She snatched up the zucchini-tainted chocolate cake – 'and using it against you as evidence. Get out of my house!'

'What's going on here?' said Mr Green, walking into that room. 'This is my house. No-one orders people out except me.'

'You can get out too!' yelled Nanny Piggins. 'Taking advantage of a woman with a head injury! You should be ashamed of yourself.'

'He took advantage of you?' asked Derrick, totally shocked.

'Yes, after you left for school this morning,' explained Nanny Piggins, 'he got me to do his laundry!'

'I thought that was within the job description of what a nanny –' began Mr Green.

'I'm going to start counting,' said Nanny Piggins. 'And when I get to three, anybody who is still in this house whom I regard to be very naughty, will get a good hard stamp on the foot. One . . .'

Nanny Anne and Mr Green both ran for it as fast as they could.

The next moment Boris burst in through the back door with a huge watermelon held above his head. 'Where is she?' asked Boris.

'There's no need to hit me over the head with a watermelon, Boris,' said Nanny Piggins.

'Aaagghh!' shrieked Boris. 'Nanny Anne has turned into a pig!'

'It's not Nanny Anne,' explained Samantha.

'Then it's one of Nanny Piggins' evil identical fourteenuplet sisters!' squealed Boris.

'No, it is I,' declared Nanny Piggins. 'Your sister, Nanny Piggins.'

'Sarah?' asked Boris, peering past the hideous hair and clothing. 'Oh no, what happened to you?'

'Nanny Anne gave me a makeover,' explained Nanny Piggins.

'You poor, poor pig,' said Boris, crushing his sister to his chest in a big bear-hug. 'What an evil woman to take advantage of you when you had come down with a little brain damage.'

'Come along, there will be plenty of time for hugging later,' said Nanny Piggins. 'We've got work to do.'

'We do?' asked Samantha.

'Getting hit in the head gave me a tremendous idea,' explained Nanny Piggins.

'It did?' asked Michael.

'Let's have a bonfire!' said Nanny Piggins. 'And burn things on it.'

'Like what?' asked Derrick.

'For a start we'll have to burn your father's Persian rug,' said Nanny Piggins. 'We'll never get the smell of zucchini out.'

'Then can we burn those clothes Nanny Anne gave you?' asked Boris.

'Definitely,' said Nanny Piggins. 'And the cake, although we'll all have to be careful to wear water-soaked rags over our noses so we don't breathe in any zucchini fumes.'

'That sounds like fun,' enthused Derrick.

'That's just the start of it,' said Nanny Piggins. 'After we've burnt your father's laundry, we'll have to stay up half the night toasting marshmallows and making up rude songs about Nanny Anne's dress sense.'

'It's good to have you back, Nanny Piggins,' said Samantha.

'It's good to be back,' said Nanny Piggins, embracing all three children. 'You've no idea how unspeakably dreadful it is not remembering the important things in life: the taste of a chocolate cake, the smell of a freshly blasted cannon and the sweet satisfaction of throwing Nanny Anne out of the house.'

CHAPTER 6

Nanny Piggins and the Bus

Sixty small noses were pressed up against the windowpanes of the school canteen, as a crowd of children breathlessly – they dared not breathe in case their breath fogged the windows – watched Nanny Piggins perform an act of sheer magic.

And this is no exaggeration. Throughout history, the world's greatest minds, people such as Leonardo da Vinci and Nicholas Flamel, have attempted alchemy – the transformation of lead into gold.

But Nanny Piggins could do something much more impressive than that. She could transform eggs, flour and butter into cake, which is much more delicious than gold, and equally pretty in Nanny Piggins' opinion.

On this particular occasion the children were waiting to see Nanny Piggins take her marble cake out of the oven. It was a mixture of white chocolate cake, milk chocolate cake and dark chocolate cake carefully swirled together. The smell coming from the oven was divine. The children could not wait to see if it looked as good as it smelt, because if it looked good and it smelt good, the chances of it tasting good were very, very high indeed.

The oven pinged. Nanny Piggins put down her romance novel (which she had been pretending to read so that the children would think she was relaxed, but really she was just as anxious to have a piece of cake as they were) and cautiously approached the oven. She sniffed the oven door.

'Definitely smells cakey,' reported Nanny Piggins.

Boris and the other canteen volunteers huddled quietly in the far corner. They knew, from experience, not to interrupt Nanny Piggins with idle chatter at such a delicate stage. Talking to Nanny Piggins as she took a cake out of the oven was like talking to a bomb disposal expert as they defused a landmine.

Nanny Piggins put on her oven gloves and carefully opened the oven door. A great waft of delicious cake smell flooded out into the kitchen and seeped through the cracks in the windowpanes. The children gasped with pleasure. (They were supposed to be in PE doing cross-country training. But when the PE teacher sent them off on a 5-kilometre run, then went back into his office to read a Dick Francis novel, he did not notice that all 60 children hid behind the girls' toilet block and then snuck around the back of the school to the canteen.)

'Hmmm,' said Nanny Piggins as she leaned forward to gently pat the top of the cake. It sprang back. 'Perfection!' she announced.

The other canteen volunteers breathed a sigh of relief.

'Congratulations Nanny Piggins, another masterpiece!' said Mrs Branston, the canteen manager.

'We mustn't speak too soon,' chided Nanny Piggins. 'It hasn't been tasted yet.'

'But you have never ever made anything less than a mouth-wateringly delicious cake,' protested Mrs Branston.

'Only because I maintain my standards,' said Nanny Piggins. 'I cannot possibly allow you to sell this cake unless it has been tasted.'

Mrs Branston sighed. They had this conversation every Tuesday when, as part of her community service, Nanny Piggins was forced to 'volunteer' in the canteen. Nanny Piggins was not always an easy pig to work with. The other mothers never threw out all the food from the freezer declaring it to be processed, chemically saturated rubbish (even though it was). The other mothers did not insist on flying in the finest ingredients from Paris. And the other mothers never chased the meat supplier off the premises just for turning up with a 10-kilogram bag of bacon.

But Mrs Branston could hardly turn Nanny Piggins away, when it was thanks to her that their school canteen had become the only school canteen in the entire world to be awarded a Michelin star. This was a recognition of culinary brilliance normally only given to the finest (and most expensive) restaurants. And the canteen only held the Michelin star on Tuesdays when it was Nanny Piggins' morning to volunteer.

It was true that having a Michelin star had caused some problems for the canteen. Food lovers and restaurant critics kept trying to get a taste of one of Nanny Piggins' creations. They would dress up as school children and sneak into line. But Nanny Piggins was very good at spotting them (usually the goatee beards and pretentious overuse of adjectives gave them away) and they all got a smack on the back of the hand with a ruler before they were sent packing.

'All right,' conceded Mrs Branston. 'Test the cake.'

Nanny Piggins turned to the children excitedly staring in through the windows. 'Are any of you children willing to be a test subject?'

'Me me me me me!!!!!!!' screamed all the children, as they did every week when Nanny Piggins would turn, with her latest creation in her trotters, and ask the same question.

Nanny Piggins began deftly slicing up the cakes (for there were 18 more in the oven) and passing them out to the children so they could give her 'constructive feedback'. The feedback was always the same. There were lots of 'Mmmm-mm-mmm' noises, and 'aaaahh-mmm-yummmm' sounds, as well as some weeping from delight.

'We're never going to make any money if you keep giving all the cake away,' said Mrs Branston.

'Who needs money when you've got cake?' argued Nanny Piggins as she shoved a large wedge into her own mouth.

Mrs Branston, who now had cake in her mouth too, had to agree that this argument did have a lot of merit. Unfortunately their cakey bliss was soon interrupted.

'What is going on here?' bellowed a very angry voice.

'It's Headmaster Pimplestock!' exclaimed Nanny Piggins.

'Quick children, run!' urged Boris.

'And take this slice of cake for your teacher,' added Nanny Piggins, 'to bribe him to concoct a cover story for you.'

The children took to their heels at lightning pace, running through an oleander hedge, along a muddy ditch, up and over the wall behind the science block and back to the oval. (So they got in their cross-country run after all.)

Headmaster Pimplestock did not chase after them because he was a rotund man who had not done anything athletic for three decades. (It is funny how adults unthinkingly inflict things on school children that they would never dream of doing themselves – like cross-country running and algebra.) Headmaster

Pimplestock glared at Nanny Piggins, which was a mistake because she was much better at it, and it always frightened him when she glared back.

'What are you doing here anyway?' asked Nanny Piggins.

'It's my school, I'm the headmaster!' exclaimed Headmaster Pimplestock.

Nanny Piggins snorted (which, as a pig, she was very good at). 'Technically I suppose,' she muttered.

Headmaster Pimplestock remembered why he was on the canteen verandah, because that was where the school noticeboard hung. (They had found that putting the notices next to that day's cake list dramatically increased the chance of the students actually reading them.) Headmaster Pimplestock walked over and pinned up a new notice.

'What does that say?' demanded Nanny Piggins.

'I don't have to answer to you,' snapped Headmaster Pimplestock.

'Really?' said Nanny Piggins, glowering so hard she actually made Headmaster Pimplestock flinch and stumble into the flowerbed.

The ladies who volunteered in the canteen (and Boris) sniggered.

Headmaster Pimplestock recovered his balance and tried to march away with dignity, but his feet would not take him. Because, after all, he was just a man, with normal human weaknesses and a sense of smell. Headmaster Pimplestock turned back. 'Umm . . . er . . . before I go . . . I was wondering, Nanny Piggins . . .'

'Tsk tsk, tsk, Headmaster,' said Nanny Piggins. 'You gave Michael lines for umming and ahhing last week, and here you are doing it yourself. Would you like me to punish you?'

'No, I would like to buy a slice of cake,' said Headmaster Pimplestock. No matter how much he desperately wanted to thwart Nanny Piggins in every way, and never see her set trotter on his school grounds again, he could not deny that her marble cake smelt like heaven in a baking tin.

'Very well,' said Nanny Piggins, cutting him a large slice and holding it out. 'That will be five hundred dollars.'

'What?' protested Headmaster Pimplestock.

'And I want to be paid in cash,' said Nanny Piggins. 'I know what you teachers are like with your rubber cheque books.'

'That's ridiculous,' spluttered Headmaster Pimplestock.

'From the very rude letter you sent Mrs Branston last week, we all know how vitally important it is that the school canteen runs at a profit,' said Nanny Piggins, pointing to a letter that was pinned to the wall (and skewered with several butter knives that Nanny Piggins had thrown at it).

'But five hundred dollars for one slice?' questioned Headmaster Pimplestock.

'You don't have to buy the cake,' said Nanny Piggins, withdrawing the outstretched plate and putting it back on the countertop.

A dollop of drool actually fell from Headmaster Pimplestock's mouth as he watched his cake get taken away. 'All right all right, no need to be hasty.' He took his wallet out of his pocket, counted out ten fifty-dollar notes and handed them to Nanny Piggins.

She handed over the cake. 'And I'd better not find out that this is the cash for the children's new axolotl tank,' warned Nanny Piggins as she put the money in the canteen till.

Headmaster Pimplestock made a mental note to put back the money for the school's axolotl tank before Nanny Piggins found out he had been using it to buy cappuccinos.

The annoying thing about Nanny Piggins was that as soon as Headmaster Pimplestock took his first bite, he had to concede that five hundred dollars was a bargain. Five *thousand* dollars would not have been too much to ask for such a delicious slice of cake. He walked away, 'Mmm-mm-mmmmm'ing and 'Aaah-mm-yummmm'ing quietly but just as fervently as the children.

Nanny Piggins, Boris and the other volunteers leaned out the window and watched him go. As soon as he was out of sight Nanny Piggins leapt out of the window and hurried over to read the sign on the noticeboard.

'What does it say?' asked Mrs Branston.

'The school wants to hire a new bus driver!' exclaimed Nanny Piggins. 'Fancy that. According to this, not only will they let the bus driver drive the bus, they will also pay them to do it. And in money.' (Nanny Piggins never had much money because Mr Green only paid her ten cents an hour. And her previous employer, the Ringmaster, had never paid her at all. So after those two it always amazed her when an employer was prepared to follow the minimum-wage laws.)

'You couldn't pay me enough to drive a bus full of kids,' said Mrs Kim, another of the volunteers. 'It's bad enough driving around my own two children, what with all the fighting and wanting snacks, and the government not letting you leave them in a car on a hot day.'

'Yes, but think of all the things you could do with a bus,' said Nanny Piggins wistfully. 'They're just so big. There is so much potential.'

'But Sarah,' said Boris, 'you can't apply. You already have a job looking after Derrick, Samantha and Michael.'

'Pish!' said Nanny Piggins. 'I can do both. I'm very good at multi-tasking. I eat cake and bake cake simultaneously all the time.'

So that afternoon Nanny Piggins went home and wrote out her job application. It was a note written in lipstick saying:

Dear School,
Please give me the job of bus driver. I know I will be better than anyone else, because I usually am at most things.
Fond Regards,
Nanny Piggins F.P. (Flying Pig)

Luckily for Nanny Piggins, Headmaster Pimplestock was not in charge of hiring the new bus driver.

There was a P&C hiring committee whose job it was to draw up a shortlist of candidates. Headmaster Pimplestock used to have full responsibility for hiring staff, but that was taken away from him when, over a 17-year period, he had only hired men (and very boring men who did not use enough deodorant).

Headmaster Pimplestock did go to the committee and beg them not to put Nanny Piggins on their shortlist, on the grounds that she was a raving psychopath who had burnt the school canteen down, blasted a hole in the library roof and bitten him on the shins several times.

But Nanny Piggins was a woman, and there were too few of them on staff. (Also, she annoyed Headmaster Pimplestock, which secretly delighted the committee.) So they overruled Headmaster Pimplestock and put Nanny Piggins on the list.

It was decided that the best way to choose a school bus driver was to hold a bus driving test. The three shortlisted candidates were summoned to the school parking lot, where they would have to navigate an obstacle course designed to test their reflexes, concentration and driving skill.

Aside from Nanny Piggins, the candidates were Mrs Thompson, the library assistant (after twenty years of waiting for the senior librarian to die so she could get a promotion, Mrs Thompson had decided the only way to further her career was to get away from books) and a neat, efficient middle-aged lady called Miss George, who actually had experience, having once been on a bus when the driver had been stung by a bee and gone into anaphylactic shock, so she'd had to commandeer the bus to drive him to the hospital.

'What do you think your chances are?' Derrick asked Nanny Piggins.

'Well I'm pretty sure I can beat Mrs Thompson, because I know for a fact she forgot her glasses, but being so timid and shy she won't have the courage to tell anyone,' said Nanny Piggins.

'But surely she won't drive the bus if she can't see,' protested Samantha.

'I think she will,' said Nanny Piggins. 'That is the extraordinary thing about shy people. They will often perform acts of supreme bravery and confidence just to get out of doing something that requires bravery and confidence.'

'What about Miss George?' asked Michael. 'She seems nice.'

'I know,' agreed Nanny Piggins, 'and having actually driven a bus before could give her an advantage.'

'All right, ladies,' called Headmaster Pimplestock. 'You will each take it in turn to drive around this obstacle course. You get 100 points if you make it around the course in less than 60 seconds. But you lose points for hitting orange cones or life-sized cardboard cut-outs of teaching staff or students.'

'How many points for a member of teaching staff?' asked Nanny Piggins.

'Five points,' said Headmaster Pimplestock.

'What? Even a maths teacher?' asked Nanny Piggins.

'Of course. They're people, aren't they?' said Headmaster Pimplestock.

'That's debatable,' muttered Derrick.

'Remember, points are bad, Nanny Piggins,' explained Samantha. 'You're not meant to hit the teachers.'

'Well, that's silly,' said Nanny Piggins. 'This game would be a lot more fun if they played it the other way round.'

'You're up first, Mrs Thompson,' called Headmaster Pimplestock.

'Good luck,' Nanny Piggins told her.

'So where are these orange cones?' Mrs Thompson asked in a whisper, as she squinted in the general direction of the course.

'They're kind of everywhere,' said Derrick.

'Oh dear,' said Mrs Thompson.

'But if it's any help to you,' added Nanny Piggins, 'the senior librarian's car is that lime green one over there.'

Mrs Thompson peered into the distance. 'Oh thank you, yes, that will do.'

Mrs Thompson got behind the wheel of the bus, turned the engine on and gunned it for the senior librarian's car. Fortunately for the senior librarian, Mrs Thompson did not know how to get the bus out of first gear, so when she hit her boss' car she was only going at eight kilometres per hour. But still, a six-tonne bus will make quite a mess of a small Japanese hatchback.

'What are you doing?' screamed Headmaster Pimplestock as he ran over to the crash site.

'Sorry,' said Mrs Thompson. 'My foot slipped on the accelerator.'

'But you steered straight for this car!' exclaimed Headmaster Pimplestock.

'My elbow locked,' explained Mrs Thompson. 'It must be my carpal tunnel from having to stamp books all day.'

Luckily the bus was of the old-fashioned solid steel variety and it sustained barely any damage at all. So it was soon Miss George's turn to demonstrate her driving skill.

'All right Miss George,' said Headmaster Pimplestock. 'Now you just have to get the bus safely round the course. Given the character deficiencies of our other applicant –' He glared meaningfully at Nanny Piggins – 'if you just get through, the job is yours.'

'Can I have the key then?' asked Miss George.

'Of course,' said Headmaster Pimplestock, handing it over.

Miss George got in the driver's seat and then began doing up her seatbelt, adjusting the mirrors and setting the radio to her favourite station.

'I don't know why you bother staying,' Headmaster Pimplestock said to Nanny Piggins. 'Miss George is obviously going to get the job.'

'Maybe,' said Nanny Piggins with a scowl. She thought Miss George was going to get the job too. But life had taught her to expect the unexpected. There was still a chance that there would be a sudden storm and a bolt of lightning would somehow find its way in through the bus' sunroof, frying Miss George at the wheel. Or a rabid squirrel could burrow up through the bus' linoleum floor and savage Miss George's ankle. You never knew.

The engine rumbled into life, and Miss George opened the driver's window. 'Headmaster?' she called.

'Yes?' replied Headmaster Pimplestock.

'I'd just like you to know,' continued Miss George, now with a big grin on her face, 'that I am a bus thief and I'm stealing your bus!'

'What the de–?!' exploded Headmaster Pimplestock.

But no-one heard what Headmaster Pimplestock said next because at that moment Miss George gunned the engine. And unlike Mrs Thompson, Miss George knew how to take the bus out of first gear and whip it up to fifth in a few seconds. She was soon blazing towards the school gates.

'Wow!' said Nanny Piggins. 'Children, this just goes to show, you should never underestimate someone. Just because they look dull and sound dull doesn't mean they aren't a crazy bus thief.'

'Stop that bus! Stop that bus!' screamed Headmaster Pimplestock as he chased after her. Though goodness knows what he thought he was doing. He was hardly going to catch up to a bus travelling at 100 kilometres an hour. And even if he did, he could hardly stop it with his bare hands. The children suspected that the only reason Headmaster Pimplestock was running after the bus was so that he could run away from Nanny Piggins and not have to see her smirk.

But fortunately for Headmaster Pimplestock, at this point something unexpected happened. When Miss George bared down on the school gates, everyone assumed she would smash right through the chain link gate. But everyone had underestimated Enrico Martinez, the school janitor.

You see, what no-one realised was that Enrico Martinez, or Dr Martinez as he was known in his own country, held a PhD in aeronautical engineering. The only reason he was working as a janitor was because during all the years he had spent learning about atmospheric pressure, structural loads and material science as it applied to propulsion, he had entirely forgotten to learn English.

And having become a janitor through necessity, he discovered that it was actually a much nicer job than being a brilliant scientist. After picking up all the rubbish and fixing the damage to the oleander hedge, there was a lot of time for drinking coffee, listening to the radio and doing crosswords.

But Enrico had become tired of replacing the school gate every time Nanny Piggins smashed through it with Mr Green's Rolls-Royce. (She had done so on several occasions. In fact, sometimes when she was annoyed with Headmaster Pimplestock she went and shut the gate just so she could drive through it to punish him.) As such, Enrico had rebuilt the school gate using the latest alloy technology and shock absorption systems.

All of which meant that when Miss George hit the school gates, instead of smashing through, the bus was actually trapped in the metal, and a remote control system immediately called the police station to report the crime.

After Miss George had been dragged away and the bus had been retrieved intact, a very smug Nanny Piggins stood in the parking lot waiting her turn to show off her driving skills.

Headmaster Pimplestock was a defeated man.

'My turn,' said Nanny Piggins with a smile. 'The key, please.'

Headmaster Pimplestock handed Nanny Piggins the key. The only comfort he took was that he had ridden a bicycle to school that day, so there was no way Nanny Piggins could damage his car.

Nanny Piggins got in the driver's seat and started the engine. Then she realised that her trotters were too short to reach the pedals.

'If you're too short to drive the bus . . .' began Headmaster Pimplestock with a spark of optimism.

'Piffle!' said Nanny Piggins. 'I'll just drive standing up.'

'But will you be able to see?' asked Samantha.

'Don't worry,' said Nanny Piggins confidently. 'I've memorised where the cones and cut-outs are.' With that she punched the accelerator with her trotter and took off.

It turns out that even though she was not a bus thief, Nanny Piggins could still drive faster than Miss George. She zipped around the course like she was driving a Lamborghini. And she did not touch one traffic cone or cardboard cut-out the whole way round – until the finish line came in sight, where there was a cardboard cut-out of Headmaster Pimplestock on the side of the road. Nanny Piggins could not resist. She swerved to drive straight over the top of it, mashing the headmaster's image into the bitumen, then righted her course and crossed the line.

'You deliberately ran me down!' complained Headmaster Pimplestock.

'Yes, but that was my only mistake so I still got 95 points,' explained Nanny Piggins happily.

'You would never drive that way in real life though, would you?' asked Headmaster Pimple-stock.

'Oh, of course not,' fibbed Nanny Piggins.

And so Nanny Piggins got the job. It came with a uniform, which Nanny Piggins immediately burnt because it was so ugly. Except for the hat. She liked the official-looking badge in the centre of the blue cap and she found she looked even more fabulous than usual if she wore it perched on her head at a jaunty angle.

The children soon found that the best thing about having their nanny become a bus driver was that there was no more waiting at the bus stop. Nanny Piggins backed the bus right into their driveway to pick them up. Then they all set off to pick up the other children.

Boris came along too. He loved riding on the bus. It was the only type of vehicle that made him feel thin.

And all the children were very pleased to see Nanny Piggins because, unlike the former bus driver, she did not have a deep hatred of children.

She actually picked up the children from *every* bus stop and waited until they had both feet inside the bus before pulling away.

Samson and Margaret Wallace were the last two children to climb aboard. Their nanny, Nanny Anne, was with them.

'Moonlighting again are you, Nanny Piggins?' she asked slyly.

'Sorry, what was that? I can't hear you,' said Nanny Piggins.

Nanny Anne stepped closer. 'I said, moonlighting again . . .'

Nanny Piggins cupped her trotter to her ear, 'Nope, can't hear you, come closer.'

Nanny Anne took another step forward. 'I said, moon—'

Nanny Piggins shut the bus door, bumping Nanny Anne's nose and making a satisfying pneumatic sound that drowned out her unsolicited advice.

'All right, is everybody aboard?' asked Nanny Piggins.

'Yep,' confirmed Samantha, double-checking the list.

'Time to go to school,' added Derrick.

'Rightio then,' said Nanny Piggins. She turned

on the engine, found first gear and adjusted her cap. 'Let's –' Nanny Piggins turned to glance at her passengers and she froze.

Nanny Anne started tapping at the window. 'What's going on?' her muffled voice demanded.

'Is something wrong, Nanny Piggins?' asked Michael.

'I can't do it,' muttered Nanny Piggins, as she looked at the 40 young faces.

'What?' asked Samantha, starting to panic. She knew it wouldn't last, her nanny was going to break the rules again.

'I can't take these children to school. I don't believe in school,' said Nanny Piggins. 'What if the teachers are planning to do something awful to them, like give them a maths test?'

The Green children looked at each other. 'Actually they are,' confessed Derrick. 'Today is the day for the school's annual standardised examinations.'

Nanny Piggins looked at the bus full of children. 'Is this true? Do you all have tests today?'

The children nodded. Except for one small girl, who had not done her homework for six months because she had secretly been watching both *The Young and The Irritable* and *The Bold and the Spiteful* in her room every night when she was supposed to be revising maths. She burst into tears.

'You poor, poor children,' sympathised Nanny Piggins. 'Don't worry, I'm here now. I'll save you!'

'What are you going to do?' wailed Samantha. She disliked standardised testing as much as the next child (seeing all those tiny boxes marked A, B, C and D made her want to be sick), but the thought of not doing them and getting zero for everything horrified her even more.

'I'm going to get you out of here,' declared Nanny Piggins, hitting the accelerator and doing a U-turn.

As they powered down the road, the children could hear the cries of Nanny Anne fading behind them as she yelled, 'Come back! You're going the wrong way!'

'Where are we going?' asked Derrick, not wanting to discourage his nanny but curious about what she had in mind.

'First we have to stop for supplies,' said Nanny Piggins.

'At an army disposals store so we can prepare for a lifetime on the run?' asked Michael.

'No, although we may do that later,' conceded Nanny Piggins. 'We have to get essential supplies first.

Which means we'll have to stop by Hans' bakery. It's Tuesday and as you know he bakes caramel éclairs on Tuesdays. We can't miss that.'

Nanny Piggins brought the bus to a screeching halt out the front of the bakery.

'All right, everybody inside. Today I am going to give you a real education, starting with maths,' announced Nanny Piggins.

The children groaned. There is something about maths – even children who are good at it don't particularly enjoy it.

'The type of maths I shall teach you today is the most essential type of maths you will ever need to know,' said Nanny Piggins. 'Even more important than how to convert your shoe size from European to North American sizes. And way, way, way more important than any of that calculus nonsense that Pythagoras fellow made up. Why he couldn't just accept that a triangle is just a triangle and get on with his life is beyond me.'

Nanny Piggins led the children inside, then got them all to empty their pockets so they could pool their money. 'Okay, now for addition. We need to add up how much we've got.'

Between the 40 children they managed to scrape together $57.

'Right,' said Nanny Piggins. 'Now the painful bit. Does anybody know how to do long division?'

'But you've always said that long division is a load of old poppycock and a waste of brain space,' said Michael.

'This is the one time that I permit it,' conceded Nanny Piggins. 'We have an important problem to work out. If éclairs are $2.80 and we have $57, how many éclairs can we buy?'

What followed was a long and protracted debate. Some of the children tried taking out paper and working it out that way. Others fogged up the glass on the cake display and did their calculations there. Then they all argued because they kept getting different results. Eventually Nanny Piggins stepped in and showed them how long division was really done. She ordered Hans to lend her his calculator and had the correct result in seconds: 20.3571.

'But how do we measure 0.3571 of a cake?' asked Michael.

'And does that mean 19.6429 of us will go without,' asked Derrick, desperately hoping he wasn't in the 19.6429.

'Of course not,' said Nanny Piggins. 'Now I shall give you a lesson in rhetoric.'

'What's rhetoric?' asked Michael.

'It's Ancient Greek for arguing,' explained Boris.

Nanny Piggins proceeded to beg, demand and cajole Hans until he could not take the onslaught anymore and just gave her forty éclairs for free (Nanny Piggins spent so much in his shop he knew he would eventually recoup the loss). Nanny Piggins then invested the $57 in doughnuts, which thankfully were $1 each and therefore the maths was much simpler.

And so the day continued. Nanny Piggins gave the children an engineering lesson by taking them to a creek and showing them how to build a dam with stones. Then she taught a biology lesson by catching tadpoles; a physics lesson by jumping high in the air and doing a bomb into the creek, splashing them all; and an English lesson by introducing them to some very colourful language when she realised she had just ruined her suede slingback shoes.

They even did a cross-country run when they heard an ice-cream van and set out after it, across a large and sticky bog. (When they caught up with the ice-cream van they remembered that they did not have any money. But now all the children knew how to do rhetoric, the ice-cream man soon caved in after being yelled at by 40 children, a pig and a bear.)

By 3.30 pm the children were exhausted from a full day of learning, and actually asked to be driven home, just so they could get some sleep. Every one of them smiled happily, and thanked Nanny Piggins for the best day at school ever (largely because they had never made it to school).

When Nanny Piggins drove the school bus home to drop off Derrick, Samantha and Michael, they found Headmaster Pimplestock outside their house, waiting for them.

'You've done it this time, Piggins,' he accused. 'You're fired, you're worse than fired. I'm going to have you arrested for kidnapping 40 children!'

'But I'm the school bus driver,' argued Nanny Piggins. 'It's my job to kidnap children. It's just that instead of taking them where they didn't want to go, I took them somewhere they did want to go – on a fun adventure with me.'

'And you can't have Nanny Piggins arrested,' added Derrick.

'Why not?' yelled Headmaster Pimplestock. 'I'd love to see her in jail. Finally we'd have some peace and quiet at the school again.'

'You'd lose your job,' explained Derrick. 'You're the one who gave the bus driving job to a pig whose trotters don't even touch the pedals . . .'

'. . . who has no respect for authority . . .' added Samantha.

'. . . and who doesn't even have a driver's licence,' finished up Michael.

'You don't have a driver's licence?' asked Headmaster Pimplestock, going pale. He was going to look very silly for not checking that.

'Of course not,' said Nanny Piggins. 'I absolutely refuse to let those people at the motor registry take my photograph. Their lighting set-up is terrible. They seem to take cruel delight in making everyone look like they've been dead for six months.'

'Well, the P&C is meeting tomorrow after school,' said Headmaster Pimplestock. 'I will be reporting to them and they can decide what to do with you.'

The P&C had a very difficult decision to make. It was true that Nanny Piggins had taken 40 students off on an impromptu excursion without obtaining the sacred passport of all off-campus activities – permission notes. However, it was also undeniable that the day after they returned, the same 40 students did extraordinarily well on their standardised testing.

The huge improvement of these students relative to their classmates could only be attributed to their having been on the most educational school excursion ever. It was quite the conundrum. In the end they reached a compromise. The committee did fire Nanny Piggins, but not for kidnapping children or her improvised school excursion. She was fired for using a fortnight's worth of petrol in one day. After all, petrol prices were expensive and the P&C could not be seen to condone their bus driver adding an extra 340 kilometres onto the journey to school every day.

But the P&C also institutionalised the annual 'Nanny Piggins Day School Excursion', where Nanny Piggins' wonderful day of adventure would be meticulously re-enacted by the entire student body for educational purposes.

CHAPTER 7

Legally Boris

Nanny Piggins and the children were sitting around the dining table, trying to ignore the fact that Mr Green was sitting with them, so they could properly enjoy the simply delicious chocolate croissants Nanny Piggins had whipped up for their breakfast. Nanny Piggins had already eaten seventeen herself, so she was beginning to slow down. Only another seven or eight and she would be full. Which meant she could now turn her attention to going through the mail.

There were the usual round of bills for Mr Green, and the usual letters for her: the Chief of NATO begging her to give him strategic advice on missile defence (Nanny Piggins always refused to help him because she knew much more about offence than defence); letters from Armani asking for fashion tips; and letters from the Slimbridge Cake Factory begging her to stop breaking into their premises and eating all the cake. Right at the bottom of the pile Nanny Piggins found a large thick envelope.

'There's a letter for Boris,' said Nanny Piggins. 'Michael, be a dear and pass it to him.'

Michael was on Boris duty that morning, which meant it was his turn to sit next to the window, passing out honey-covered croissants. Mr Green still had not realised he had a ten-foot-tall 700-kilogram dancing bear living in his garden shed, which is why this little subterfuge was necessary.

As the envelope passed out the window, the sound of Boris gobbling food abruptly stopped.

Mr Green looked up from his newspaper. 'Ah thank goodness, Mrs Simpson has stopped using her wood chipper.'

'Why yes,' said Nanny Piggins. (She had told Mr Green that the loud noises they heard every breakfast time were because Mrs Simpson spent every morning making wood chips.)

But a moment later there was a loud noise that was much harder to explain.

'Whooppeee!' yelled Boris.

'What was that?' asked Mr Green, looking up from the financial pages again.

'It was just me,' fibbed Nanny Piggins, as she leapt up and hastily drew the curtains. 'I yelled "whooppeee" because I'm so happy to be alive.'

'Well, stop it,' said Mr Green grumpily before returning his attention to the newspaper. Reading the stock listings always took his full concentration. His brain was not good at multi-tasking (it was not good at single-tasking either).

'Hooray! Hooray!' sang Boris delightedly from the garden.

Nanny Piggins and the children exchanged glances. If Boris was going to remain a secret they would have to get Mr Green out of the house immediately. Unfortunately Nanny Piggins could not think of a subtle way to do this, so she would have to resort to less sophisticated methods.

'Get out!' screamed Nanny Piggins as she grabbed Mr Green and started dragging him towards the front door.

'What's the meaning of this?' demanded Mr Green.

'Nanny Piggins just wants you to get to the office nice and early,' fabricated Samantha, 'in case the government issued amendments to the tax codes during the night and you inadvertently started breaking the law while you slept.'

'They didn't, did they?' asked Mr Green, turning white and beginning to hurry towards the door voluntarily.

'Who knows?' said Michael. 'A lady from the tax office did ring and ask me to read out all the papers I could find in your briefcase.'

'What?' yelped Mr Green as he took off running without his jacket, shoes or briefcase.

As he yanked open the front door Mr Green had a brief moment of clarity and turned back. 'My briefcase?' he asked.

'Don't worry,' said Nanny Piggins. 'We'll run it through Mrs Simpson's wood chipper. The tax office won't be able to prove a thing.'

'Thank you,' gushed Mr Green, before running barefoot down the street.

'That was fun,' said Nanny Piggins. 'Now let's see what Boris is doing in the garden.'

As Nanny Piggins and the children stepped out into the backyard they were greeted by a spectacular sight. It was a beautiful spring morning, dew was still on the grass, and beams of light cut through the leaves of the trees like rays of magic reaching down from heaven. But most spectacular of all was Boris as he leapt, pranced and pirouetted across the lawn, only occasionally banging into the compost bin or landing on a geranium because he was so caught up in the emotion of the moment.

'Boris seems very happy,' said Samantha. 'What do you suppose his letter was about?'

'Who knows?' said Nanny Piggins. 'Perhaps someone died and left him a lifetime supply of honey.'

'Does he know any sick elderly people with that much honey?' asked Derrick.

'No,' admitted Nanny Piggins, 'but he does try to meet people like that all the time.'

Knowing it was rude to interrupt a maestro in full flow of creative genius, Nanny Piggins and the children stood and watched for twenty minutes. Eventually, after a flurry of grand jetés, a couple of pirouettes and some spinning high kicks, Boris collapsed dramatically on the ground, landing in the splits.

Nanny Piggins and the children burst into applause.

'Bravo!' called Derrick.

'Encore!' yelled Samantha.

'Would you like another honey-covered croissant?' called Michael, who knew his favourite bear well and had six honey-covered croissants at the ready.

'Yes, please!' exclaimed Boris, leaping up again and bounding over to the children.

'So what was your letter about? It's obviously made you very happy,' said Nanny Piggins.

'Mmmayotinawwool,' said Boris. (It is hard to enunciate with croissants in your mouth.)

'I beg your pardon?' asked Nanny Piggins. 'Admittedly I'm not as fluent in bear-with-his-mouth-full as I probably should be, but it sounded like you said "I got into law school".'

'I did!' exclaimed Boris, after swallowing. 'I got a letter saying I had been accepted. I start on Monday.'

Nanny Piggins and the children were astonished.

'Really? What sort of law school?' asked Derrick, suspecting Boris of applying to some institution he had seen advertised at a bus stop.

'See for yourself,' said Boris, proudly handing Derrick the letter.

'Leaping Lamingtons!' exclaimed Derrick. (He had picked up this expression from Nanny Piggins.) 'He's been accepted into the most prestigious university in the country!'

'Let me smell that,' said Nanny Piggins, taking the letter from Derrick and giving it a good sniff. 'It doesn't smell like one of the Ringmaster's tricks.'

'That's because it isn't,' said Boris proudly. 'I filled in all the forms, wrote all the essays and even snuck out for an interview last week without telling anyone. I don't like to be secretive, but I thought it important not to get all your hopes up.'

The children did not know what to say. The idea of Boris being accepted into any sort of law school, let alone the most prestigious one in the country, was just so extraordinary. Samantha gathered her thoughts first.

'No offence, Boris, because you know we all love you, and we all think you are a wonderful genius,' said Samantha, 'but *why* did the university accept you? You aren't exactly . . . um . . . the academic type.'

'I know,' admitted Boris. 'I believe they were under some pressure to accept more minorities. And since I'm Russian, I'm a bear and I didn't go to private school, I was a minority in three different ways.'

'And again, no offence Boris, but isn't law a post-graduate degree?' asked Derrick. 'Don't you have to have a regular degree already in order to apply?'

'But I do have a university degree,' said Boris.

'You do?' exclaimed Nanny Piggins. 'You never told me that.'

'Well, I don't like to brag,' said Boris, 'and I know you are still upset with Cambridge University for refusing to give you an honorary doctorate in cake baking.'

'It is snubs like that that turn pigs like me into evil geniuses living under volcanoes and thinking up ways to take over the world,' grumbled Nanny Piggins.

'I know,' said Boris sympathetically. 'But I did a Masters degree in Applied Ballet years ago, while I was still living in Russia.'

'What's *Applied Ballet?*' asked Derrick.

'It's the use of ballet to facilitate change in everyday situations,' explained Boris. 'Like using ballet to disband an angry mob. Or using ballet to inspire scientists to come up with a cure for the common cold.'

'What sort of university would give a degree in that?' asked Michael.

'Only the best,' said Boris. 'Moscow University. They take ballet very seriously. Everyone who studies there has to know dance. Even doctors and lawyers have to be able to skip about on their tippy-toes or they aren't allowed to graduate.'

'It sounds like a very sensible institution,' said Nanny Piggins. 'So many universities clog young people's heads with rubbish about post-modernism, cultural studies and mathematics; it's nice to know there is still somewhere you can go to get a proper education. But what I want to know is – why did you apply to law school? I thought you were happy here. I had no idea you wanted to further your education.'

'Oh goodness me, no,' said Boris. 'I'm as averse to education as the next bear. You know how learning new things hurts my head sometimes.'

'It took you three weeks to understand that Bethany had secretly had a surrogate child with Bridge's twin brother's father on *The Young and the Irritable*,' said Samantha.

'Exactly,' agreed Boris. 'But I wanted to do something to help you, Sarah. And it seems to me it will be quicker for me to go to law school, qualify as a barrister and get you off in a dramatic court-room showdown than for you to actually finish your community service hours.'

'You would do all that for me?' said Nanny Piggins, a tear of gratitude beginning to well in her eye. 'You are the kindest, sweetest brother a pig could ever have.'

And with that she gave her brother the biggest pig hug ever (a pig hug is not quite as big as a bear hug because pigs have much shorter arms, but when it comes to hugging, it is the squeezing that counts and Nanny Piggins put in lots of extra squeeze). Then they all went inside to have honey-covered pikelets to celebrate.

When Monday morning came around Boris was all ready for his first day at university. His fur was brushed, his pencils were sharpened and Nanny Piggins had even borrowed Mr Green's ugliest bow tie for him to wear.

'Brainy people always think bow ties look good,' explained Nanny Piggins. 'I think it's because the brainy part of their brain is so swollen it crushes the part of the brain that would usually give them fashion sense.'

'I'm a little nervous,' admitted Boris. 'What if none of the other law students will play with me at lunchtime?'

'I don't think law students do play at lunch-time,' said Derrick. 'I think they read law books or sit around having intellectual debates about hypothetical law cases.'

'That sounds awful,' panicked Boris. 'Couldn't I read a nice comic book instead? I've got three lectures this morning, so by the time lunch comes around my brain will need to put its feet up and have a rest.'

'Why don't you just do some ballet at lunch-time,' suggested Nanny Piggins. 'No-one will be able to question your cultural superiority once they see you do your interpretation of a dying swan.'

The children were not as confident as Nanny Piggins in Boris' ability to win over a bunch of pretentious intellectual law students through ballet alone. But they decided to stay silent so as not to make him any more nervous on his first day.

That afternoon, when the children came home from school, they found Nanny Piggins already in the kitchen baking.

'You're back early,' observed Derrick. 'Weren't you meant to be cleaning graffiti off walls for your community service?'

'The supervisor asked me to leave,' said Nanny Piggins.

'Why?' asked Samantha.

'All I did was suggest that instead of painting over the graffiti, it might be nicer to add to it,' said Nanny Piggins, 'which I demonstrated by turning a spray painting of a very rude word into a replica of Van Gogh's sunflowers.'

'Oh,' said Samantha.

'She yelled at me and told me to whitewash over it,' continued Nanny Piggins, 'but when I started, passers-by protested because my painting was so pretty. It almost started a riot. So I was sent home.'

'You do seem to have a knack for getting early marks from community service,' said Michael.

'I know,' agreed Nanny Piggins. 'I don't think the system is set up to deal with someone of my creative genius. Which makes it very difficult for me to log up my hours.'

Just then Boris returned.

'How was your first day at law school?' asked Nanny Piggins.

'Very refreshing,' said Boris happily.

'Really?' said Nanny Piggins. 'I thought it would be stodgy and boring, with lots of tedious, hard-to-understand things being explained badly by men with bad breath.'

'That's exactly what it was like,' agreed Boris happily. 'Each lecture I walked into put me to sleep in seconds. I had four of the loveliest naps I've ever had.'

'But did you learn anything?' asked Michael.

'Oh yes,' said Boris. 'I learnt it is not a good idea to do ballet in the quadrangle at lunchtime. Not when the theatre students are holding their fire-breathing workshop.'

'They set you on fire?' asked an alarmed Samantha.

'Only my bottom,' said Boris. 'Luckily there was a fish pond nearby so I was able to grand jeté into it immediately. Which made a spectacular end to my performance.'

'Anyway, I'd better go and take my new law books out to the shed,' said Boris. 'They don't have very pretty covers, so I thought I'd cut the covers off more exciting books and glue them over. I don't want people on the bus to think I'm boring, otherwise they may not gossip with me.'

'Very wise,' approved Nanny Piggins as her brother left the room. 'Boris seems to be adjusting to law school very well.'

The children were not so sure. Nanny Piggins had no formal education herself, so she did not really understand that people like teachers and law professors were usually not open-minded enough to appreciate the benefits of a student sleeping through everything they said.

Boris continued to go to law school for another two weeks, and he had never been so refreshed in his life. He had even started taking a pillow with him so he could get extra comfortable for his naps. But halfway through his third week, trouble struck.

Nanny Piggins and the children were at home hiding in the cellar (trying to evade the probation officer who wanted her to go down to the docks and help clean up an oil spill) when the phone rang.

'If we answer it the probation officer will know we're here,' said Nanny Piggins.

'He already knows we're here because he saw you in the front garden,' Derrick pointed out.

'And he heard you yell, "Quick, hide in the cellar. I don't want to clean up an oil spill, I've got a lovely frock on," ' said Samantha.

'I'll answer the phone,' volunteered Michael. 'If the probation officer sees me through the window I'll tell him you're really one of your own identical twin sisters.'

'Good thinking,' said Nanny Piggins. 'They're always stealing my identity. It won't do any harm if I borrow one of theirs for half an hour.'

A few moments later, Michael ran back down the cellar steps carrying the phone. 'It's an emergency,' he cried. 'Boris has fallen into one of his super deep hibernation sleeps in the doorway of a lecture theatre and none of the other students can get out.'

'Aren't there windows they can climb through?' asked Nanny Piggins.

'It's a five-storey building,' explained Michael. 'They'd fall to their deaths.'

'Oh well, I suppose we had better go and sort him out,' said Nanny Piggins.

'What about the probation officer?' asked Samantha. 'If you leave he'll grab you.'

'Luckily I had the foresight to anticipate this sort of situation,' said Nanny Piggins. 'I've rigged up a flying fox on the roof. We'll be able to whiz past over his head without him even knowing.'

When Nanny Piggins and the children arrived at the lecture hall there was quite a crowd gathered. University students enjoy any excuse to stand around and gawp rather than go to their lectures, and there were lots of very concerned university staff and two fire trucks in attendance as well.

'Hello Fire Chief!' called Nanny Piggins to her old friend. He had been called out many times to deal with fires caused by her frequent kitchen- or cannon-related explosions.

'Hello Nanny Piggins,' said the Fire Chief. 'I don't suppose you've brought any . . .' he paused and looked at Nanny Piggins optimistically. (Technically, as Fire Chief, he wasn't allowed to ask for bribes.)

'Any cake?' prompted Nanny Piggins. 'Why yes, of course, I never leave home without supplies. Would you and your men like some chocolate cake?'

'Yes, please,' chorused the firefighters.

'Um, Ms Piggins,' said a nervous elderly man, 'I'm the Vice Chancellor of the university.'

'Oh, I'm sorry,' said Nanny Piggins. 'I've got a friend who runs a bakery. Do you want me to ask him if he'll give you a proper job?'

'No, thank you,' said the Vice Chancellor. 'I was just wondering if you would be so kind as to do something about your brother. The head of the university's veterinary school is frightened to wake him up because he has no practical experience with tired Kodiak bears.'

'There's no need to worry,' said Nanny Piggins. 'My brother would never hurt anyone under any circumstances, unless you tried to eat one of his honey sandwiches. Then he would snap you in two like a dry twig. But that doesn't happen very often. Who would eat a bear's honey sandwich?'

Nanny Piggins went over to where of Boris' back entirely blocked the exit.

'How did he manage to fall asleep right in the doorway?' asked Nanny Piggins.

'Apparently the lecture had started just before he arrived,' explained the Vice Chancellor, 'so as soon as he entered the room the sound of the professor's voice sent him into an immediate sleep.'

'Hmm, yes,' said Nanny Piggins. 'The exact same thing happens to me whenever I hear people talk about cricket. It's such a shame. Cricket bats are so useful for whacking things. Why must people insist on using them for actual cricket?'

'Um, your brother?' reminded the Vice Chancellor.

'Oh, of course,' said Nanny Piggins, turning to look at Boris' back.

'How are you going to wake him up?' asked Derrick. 'Are you going to ask the Fire Chief to lend you one of his super high-powered hoses?'

'That would work,' agreed Nanny Piggins, 'but we better not. We wouldn't want to ruin the carpet. It is a hideous brown–green colour as it is. Making it waterlogged would only make it worse. No, I have another idea.'

Nanny Piggins went right up to Boris, took a deep breath and yelled clearly, 'Rudolph Nureyev was the world's best ballet dancer!' Then she hurriedly took several steps back.

Nothing happened.

'What good was that supposed to do?' asked the bewildered Vice Chancellor.

'Just wait,' said Nanny Piggins.

Suddenly Boris leapt to his feet. 'Rudolph Nureyev was a great big show-off!' he yelled. 'He wouldn't know how to *plié* properly if he broke his foot and had it reset at a right angle.'

'Oh Boris, I'm so dreadfully sorry to have to say such a hateful thing,' apologised Nanny Piggins. 'I only did it to wake you up.'

'Oh, that's all right, Sarah,' said Boris kindly, clutching his heart as he recovered from the shock. 'I was just terrified for a moment that I had fallen asleep and woken up in a parallel universe where people really thought Rudolph Nureyev was better than me.'

'No-one could possibly think that,' Nanny Piggins assured him, 'except all those ballet critics and aficionados. But what would they know? I think blood clots have gone to their brains from all the time they spend sitting in cramped theatre seats.'

'Right, that's it!' screamed a voice from inside the lecture theatre.

'Oh dear,' said Boris. 'It sounds like my Constitutional Law professor is upset about something.'

And indeed he was.

'I am not putting up with this for another day!' yelled the Constitutional Law professor as he pushed past Boris and confronted the Vice Chancellor. 'I don't care about your minority quotas. I absolutely refuse to put up with this bear snoring his way through another one of my lectures.'

'I don't snore!' protested Boris. 'Do I?' He turned to look at his fellow students now filing out of the lecture theatre. The students nodded sheepishly.

'But only a little bit,' a nice young student assured him. 'And we don't mind, because it often drowns out the more boring bits of the lecture.'

'It is disrespectful, disgraceful, disruptive and a complete waste of everyone's time,' yelled the Constitutional Law professor.

'Just like studying Constitutional Law,' whispered Nanny Piggins.

'I heard that!' screamed the Constitutional Law professor. 'I want this bear thrown out. I refuse to teach him for another day.'

'Um . . .' said the Vice Chancellor. He did not like to make decisions at the best of times. But certainly not when there were a couple of hundred students, two dozen firefighters and a variety of his staff looking at him. 'To expel a student who has not failed any exams or committed any crime is very difficult.'

'He has slept through every single lecture,' yelled the Constitutional Law professor. 'He has been here two and a half weeks and hasn't heard a single word I've said.'

'Lucky Boris,' whispered one of the students.

'I heard that!' yelled the professor.

'Well, if you want him to be removed there will have to be a full academic hearing,' said the Vice Chancellor.

'Fine,' snapped the law professor. 'How soon can it be arranged?'

'Um . . .' said the Vice Chancellor, 'perhaps next semester?'

'Tomorrow, I insist tomorrow,' yelled the law professor, the veins in his forehead starting to stick out most alarmingly.

'Um, all right,' said the Vice Chancellor. 'After lunch.'

'And a nap?' asked Boris hopefully.

And so the next day they all regathered at the university, but this time in the Great Hall. (A great big room with fancy stonework and stained glass, usually reserved for intimidating students at exam time or graduations.) Up on the stage was a long table where a line of senior academics sat, wearing their black gowns and silly flat hats.

In front of the stage there was an unexpectedly large audience – partly because it was a rainy day, so a lot of students were looking for somewhere dry to eat their lunch. But as well as that, Boris actually did have a lot of supporters. Because he slept through every lecture he did not realise how many friends he'd made. Students who forgot to bring a jumper on cold days would snuggle up to him to stay warm; students who forgot to bring a pencil would borrow one of Boris' as they lay untouched on his desk; and students who had not done the required reading would fight to sit behind Boris' ten-foot-tall frame so that the lecturer would not see them and ask a difficult question.

Even many of the professors had turned out to support Boris. They liked having a student who never asked awkward questions or complained about the due dates of assignments. He always greeted the assignment schedule as a welcome surprise when he woke up from a nap and found one of his fellow students had sticky-taped a copy to his forehead.

'Now, are you sure you want to go through with this?' Nanny Piggins whispered to her brother as they sat in the front row, waiting for the hearing to start. 'Personally I'm looking forward to yelling at all these silly academics and perhaps biting a few shins. But I know how you hate confrontation, so if you'd rather run away and try to find a broom closet big enough for you to hide in, I'd totally understand.'

'No, it's all right, Sarah, I do want to do this,' said Boris, steeling himself to be brave. 'I like coming to law school. It makes a nice change from my shed. And I've only got three years and forty-nine weeks to go, so it would be a terrible shame to drop out now.'

Just then, at the back of the hall, the Chancellor entered. A hush came over the crowd. (You have to understand that at a university it is the Vice Chancellor who really runs things. The Chancellor's role is more like the Queen, largely ceremonial, but technically she does have ultimate power when something very important happens. So as the Chancellor entered the hall everybody, including the withered old academics, stood up as a mark of respect.)

The Chancellor made her way up onto the stage and sat at the middle of the long table. The crowd waited for her to start proceedings, as she readjusted her academic gown and rustled about in her handbag for a cough drop. Finally she found one, popped it in her mouth, then looked up at the audience.

'Before we begin,' said the Chancellor with a quavery voice, 'I would just like to say that I have been an academic for 63 years and as such, I resent anything that requires me to get out of bed before eleven.'

'I like this woman,' said Nanny Piggins, nodding. 'She is clearly very clever.'

'I do not want to be here,' continued the Chancellor. 'After six decades of studying the molecular structure of quarks, I feel that I am entitled to sit in my study and watch *The Young and the Irritable* undisturbed.'

'Here, here!' yelled Nanny Piggins.

The Chancellor paused. 'Vice Chancellor, why is there a pig in the front row of the audience?'

'Because her brother, the bear, is the one we are here about,' explained the Vice Chancellor.

The Chancellor put on her reading glasses and peered over the edge of the high table at Boris. She sighed. 'Oh well, I suppose admission criteria have changed since my day.'

'Perhaps we should start the proceedings?' suggested the Vice Chancellor.

'Yes, yes,' agreed the Chancellor. 'Who is going to be complaining today?'

'I am,' said the professor of Constitutional Law, leaping to his feet. 'I want this bear expelled immediately. He has shown no interest in or aptitude for the law. In fact he has slept through every moment of every one of my lectures.'

'Hmm,' said the Chancellor. 'But aren't we supposed to be encouraging diversity on campus? If we are meant to encourage minorities, why not encourage the very tired? I know I feel very tired all the time and I often feel like I'm a minority.'

'But if he sleeps through every lecture,' said the professor, 'he will fail his exams, so why waste everyone's time struggling through an entire semester of his incessant snoring. He should be expelled now.'

'What do you have to say for yourself?' the Chancellor asked, peering over her glasses at Boris.

Boris rose to his feet, opened his mouth, then promptly burst into tears and collapsed in his seat.

Nanny Piggins leapt up as Samantha hugged Boris reassuringly.

'You will have to excuse my brother,' said Nanny Piggins. 'He is Russian and a ballet dancer and therefore twice as in touch with his emotions as regular people.'

'That's quite all right,' said the Chancellor. 'I often feel like bursting into tears at university functions. Although in my case it is usually through sheer boredom from having to listen to the world's most tedious speeches.'

'In my brother's defence, I would like to say a few words,' said Nanny Piggins.

'Please go ahead,' said the Chancellor.

'Well, first of all I'd like to point out that that man –' said Nanny Piggins as she pointed dramatically at the professor of Constitutional Law – 'is a big poopy head. I'm sorry to have to resort to such colourful language but there is no other way to express the depths of my feelings. He is a meany. And a bully. And very ungenerous to my sweet and caring brother. Furthermore, if he does get Boris thrown out of university on some minor sleep-related technicality, then I shall be forced to give both his shins a good hard bite!'

'Did you hear that?' exclaimed the professor of Constitutional Law. 'She threatened me with physical violence!'

'I heard it,' admitted the Chancellor, 'and I must say it made a refreshing change. Although it does make me inclined to decide in your favour, because I'd like to see her bite you.'

'This is an outrage, it's preposterous –' spluttered the professor.

'Oh shut up,' said the Chancellor.

'You tell him!' encouraged Nanny Piggins.

'Thank you,' said the Chancellor. 'It seems to me a very simple matter. The bear wants to stay because he wants to study law. Is that right?'

Boris dabbed his eyes, sniffed and nodded.

'But you want to throw him out because he sleeps through every lecture and hasn't learnt anything. Is that right?' the Chancellor asked the professor.

'Precisely. The notion of allowing a –' began the professor.

'Just say "yes" or "no", or I'll throw you out instead,' warned the Chancellor.

'Yes,' said the professor (which was the shortest sentence he had uttered since he had turned two).

'Well then, if you can prove that the bear knows nothing you have taught in the last three weeks, I will agree to expel him,' said the Chancellor. 'So fire away. Give the bear a pop quiz.'

'All right,' said the professor as he turned to Boris with a malicious gleam in his eye. 'Define sub judice.'

Boris whispered to Samantha, 'What does "define" mean?'

'Explain the meaning,' said Samantha.

'Oh,' said Boris. He stood up, cleared his throat and began, 'Um . . . er . . . ahem.'

'He doesn't know,' said the professor gleefully.

'Yes I do. It's all about honey,' said Boris.

'No it's not,' said the professor.

'It is the way I remember it,' said Boris. 'You see, if a bear was accused of stealing a big bucket of honey, no-one could mention how all bears have an insatiable lust for big buckets of honey – at least, not until after the case was over, otherwise it could influence the judge's decision. And judges don't like that. It makes them yell at you. Because of sub judice.'

'Was that the right answer?' the Chancellor asked the very old law professor sitting to her left.

'Yes,' said the elderly professor. 'Couldn't have put it better myself.'

'He just got lucky,' scoffed the professor of Constitutional Law. 'I'll try another one. Explain *habeas corpus*.'

'Oh, I know that one too,' said Boris. 'It is just like that episode of *The Young and the Irritable* where Bethany became the Chief of Police and she had Bridge arrested on trumped-up bootlegging charges, to punish him for refusing to take her to the annual policepersons' ball. As soon as Bridge was arrested he was brought before a magistrate, who realised that the charges were silly when Bethany burst into tears and revealed just how much she loved him. That's why you have *habeas corpus* – to protect people from being unfairly arrested.'

'I remember that episode,' said the Chancellor. 'It was a good one.'

'You should consider fast-tracking this fellow for a professorship,' said the elderly law professor. 'He clearly has a brilliant legal mind.'

The law students in the audience were nodding their agreement. Boris had explained the complicated legal ideas much better than their professor. It was the first time they had understood these concepts properly themselves.

'When is *mens rea* of primary importance in the determination of a conviction?' spat the Constitutional Law professor.

'Hang on,' cried a law student in the audience, 'that hasn't been covered in any of our lectures.'

'It's all right, I know because it's about honey too,' said Boris. 'You know how when someone leaves a slice of honey-covered toast on the kitchen bench, sometimes it can end up in your mouth accidentally? You didn't mean to eat the toast, it just happened. Well that's not so bad because there was no *mens rea*. You didn't mean to do it.'

'How do you know that if it wasn't in your lectures?' asked the Chancellor.

'I read it in a book,' explained Boris.

'Which book?' asked Nanny Piggins.

'Well, I've been getting so much sleep in the daytime during lectures,' explained Boris, 'that I've been finding it very difficult to get to sleep at night. So I've been reading my law textbooks to try to put myself to sleep.'

'And you remember everything you read?' marvelled the Chancellor.

'Oh yes,' said Boris. 'Bears have excellent memory retention. I think it's because we don't have to go to school. Our heads are much emptier than the average human's, which means there is a lot of room to put things.'

'How do you explain knowing everything that was covered in your lectures?' asked the Chancellor.

'Well, just because I'm asleep doesn't mean I'm not listening,' said Boris. 'That would be rude. Since we bears sleep so much in winter we have learnt to listen while we sleep. Otherwise we would miss three months of episodes of *The Young and the Irritable* and it would be impossible to catch up.'

'Very well,' said the Chancellor. 'It seems to me that my decision is clear. The bear can stay.'

'Hooray!' cheered everyone in the audience. Boris burst into tears again.

'But what about the snoring?!' protested the professor of Constitutional Law.

'I think it will do you good,' said the Chancellor. 'You should see it as a challenge. You need to try to make your lectures more interesting to listen to than a bear's snores.'

Nanny Piggins piped up. 'Aren't you going to censure the professor for anti-sleepism and bearist behaviour?'

'That's a good idea,' agreed the Chancellor. 'I do want to send a message to the rest of the teaching staff not to waste my time with this sort of charade. All right, I'm giving you an official warning for discriminatory behaviour towards the sleeping.'

'Hooray!' cheered the audience again.

Boris' fellow law students then tried to carry him triumphantly out into the quadrangle on their shoulders, but they had to give up when they realised they could not lift him. So instead Boris danced out into the quadrangle and treated everyone to an impromptu performance of the ballet *Don Quixote*, which was so good that even the Chancellor delayed her return to her video-taped episode of *The Young and the Irritable* so she could watch him.

CHAPTER 8

Nanny Piggins and the Last Straw

Nanny Piggins had suffered a terrible personal tragedy. She was in the middle of making zabaglione ice-cream (zabaglione is Italian for 'even more delicious custard') when an electricity substation three blocks away had caught fire, causing everyone in a five kilometre radius to lose all power to their houses.

Now normally Nanny Piggins enjoyed a good blackout. It was an excellent excuse to light lots of candles and tell ghost stories. But Nanny Piggins did not enjoy a blackout when she was making ice-cream, because she had an electric powered ice-cream maker.

She tried running next door to Mrs Simpson's house, but of course her power was out too. So she ran the ice-cream maker around to the Retired Army Colonel's house (his legs had finally healed and he had been able to escape the nursing home), in the hopes that he had a generator. But he did not.

So Nanny Piggins had been forced to sit on the curb, weeping and eating the unfrozen zabaglione to console herself. Eventually the delicious custard gave her the strength to compose herself and, summoning the spirit of Scarlet O'Hara (a woman so bold she could have been a pig), she rose to her trotters and declared, 'As God is my witness I shall never eat unfrozen ice-cream again.'

This is how she and the children came to be making their house energy self-sufficient by sticky-taping solar panels to their roof.

'Why are we using sticky tape?' asked Derrick. 'Wouldn't it be better to use an electric screw-driver?'

'I don't think the structure of the roof could take it,' explained Nanny Piggins. 'It was pretty rotten and unsound to start with, due to your father's lack of repairs. But Boris has fallen through the roof seven times now.'

'Eight,' Boris reminded her.

'Oh, yes. I forgot the time you fell through the roof while trying to adjust the television aerial to pick up Russian soap operas,' agreed Nanny Piggins. 'So actually sticky-taping solar panels to the house will improve the structural soundness, like an exoskeleton on an insect.'

Just then they heard the screech of tyres as a speeding car skidded around the corner and raced down their street.

'Isn't that Mr Green's vomit-yellow Rolls-Royce?' asked Boris.

Nanny Piggins and the children turned and looked down at the street.

'What on earth is he doing, driving like a lunatic?' wondered Derrick.

'He must have had a brain aneurism,' declared Nanny Piggins. 'I've heard about these things – some people have brain aneurisms and then suddenly find they can speak French. Your father must have had an aneurism and suddenly found he can drive properly.'

They watched Mr Green leap out of his car and run to the front door (always a funny sight because he was a rotund man and he did tend to wobble when he moved quickly). Then they heard him rushing from room to room.

'I wonder what he's doing?' said Michael.

'Perhaps he's been given a tip-off that the police are going to arrest him for tax evasion so he is desperately looking for a clean pair of underwear,' guessed Nanny Piggins.

'Why would he need a clean pair of underwear if he is being raided?' asked Samantha.

'I've heard police searches can be very thorough,' explained Nanny Piggins.

Just then Mr Green burst out into the backyard. 'Piggins! Where are you?' he cried.

'Piggins?' said Nanny Piggins. 'Do you think it is me he is referring to in that rude way?'

'I can't imagine why he would be calling out to one of your thirteen identical twin sisters or Bramwell,' said Derrick.

'Up here,' called Nanny Piggins.

Mr Green turned and looked up at the roof. 'Get down immediately,' he barked.

'What did he eat for breakfast this morning?' Nanny Piggins asked the children. 'Whatever it was, remind me to throw the box out. It has made him unpleasantly forceful.'

Nanny Piggins and the children climbed down the wisteria vine to the garden, while Boris hid behind the chimney stack, pretending to be a nesting pigeon by saying 'coo coo'.

From his rushing about and yelling, the children had expected their father to be angry about something, but when they reached the ground and could see his face they realised that he was excited. Very excited.

'What's going on?' asked Nanny Piggins.

'Silence!' ordered Mr Green. 'I don't have to put up with any more impertinence, insubordination or threats from you.'

'I think it's the muesli,' decided Nanny Piggins. 'All that fibre has finally made his brain snap.'

'Shut up!' yelled Mr Green.

The children gasped. Even Nanny Piggins was stunned into silence. She had never heard Mr Green say anything so brave before. After all, no-one knew better than he how hard Nanny Piggins could bite a shin.

'When I got to work this morning I found everyone laughing at me,' said Mr Green.

'Well, it is Monday,' said Nanny Piggins.

'Be quiet!' said Mr Green. 'They were laughing at me because one of the secretaries had been reading a court circular and noticed your name. You have been convicted of a criminal offence and sentenced to 5000 hours community service, haven't you?'

'Technically, yes,' conceded Nanny Piggins.

'But that was months ago,' said Derrick. 'You only found out now?'

'You can shut up too!' yelled Mr Green.

'Do not speak to your children that way,' said Nanny Piggins, beginning to glower.

'I will speak to my children any way I want,' said Mr Green, smirking, 'and I don't have to listen to you a moment longer, because you've gone too far this time. It's bad enough that you are a pig, but I cannot be expected to employ a pig with a criminal record.'

'But all Nanny Piggins did was tightrope walk between two buildings so she could have a slice of chocolate cake,' protested Michael.

'I don't care!' yelled Mr Green. 'She has a criminal record. That is grounds for termination of her employment. No employment tribunal in the world would expect me to let a criminal look after my children.'

'What are you saying?' asked Nanny Piggins. She was finding it hard to follow because she did tend to tune out when Mr Green started using multisyllabic words.

'I'm saying you are fired! You're sacked! Your services are no longer required!' yelled Mr Green gleefully. 'I want you to get out of my house right now and never darken my doorstep again!'

'But Father, you can't fire Nanny Piggins,' said Samantha, tears streaming down her face. 'If she goes you'll have to look after us yourself.'

'Ah, that's where you're wrong,' said Mr Green. 'Times have changed. I won't have to spend time with you at all.'

'Be careful, children,' warned Nanny Piggins. 'I think he's been reading *Lord of the Flies* and he's planning to abandon you on a desert island. And I mean desert as in "an empty wasteland", and not dessert as in "pudding", so don't get excited.'

'No, I've got something even better in mind,' cackled Mr Green. 'Thanks to modern technology I can get video cameras installed in every room in the house and watch you on my computer monitor at work without ever leaving my desk.'

'That's crazy,' said Derrick.

'Crazy or brilliant?' said Mr Green triumphantly.

'Definitely crazy,' said Nanny Piggins.

'Well that's the way it's going to be,' said Mr Green, before turning on Nanny Piggins, 'so you can get out of this house right now!'

Nanny Piggins did not move. She just glowered.

'Fine,' said Mr Green. 'I'm happy to call the police and add trespassing to your criminal record.'

Nanny Piggins growled.

'Yes, I'll be sure to report that too,' said Mr Green. 'Making threats.'

'You'd better go,' said Derrick to Nanny Piggins. 'We don't want you to get in trouble.'

'I can't leave you with this dreadful man,' said Nanny Piggins, as she sized up Mr Green's shins.

'We'll be all right,' sobbed Samantha. 'You'll always be with us in our hearts.'

'What do you mean?' asked Nanny Piggins. 'I know I'm not terribly tall, but I can't see how I could possibly fit inside your heart cavity. And even if I did I don't think it would be a good place for me to stay. You've got lots of important valves and ventricles in there, and it's best if they are left well alone.'

'Samantha means that even if you're gone, we'll always love you,' explained Michael.

Now Nanny Piggins started to cry. 'I love you too,' she declared, giving them all an enormous group hug.

Mr Green rolled his eyes. 'This is more sickening than watching one of those dreadful daytime soap operas.'

'Right, that's it! I'm biting him!' declared Nanny Piggins. 'It is one thing for you to fire me and ruin the lives of your own children, but how dare you insult the finest television programming our screens have to offer!'

Fortunately the children were able to grab Nanny Piggins and, with considerable coaxing (and lots of cake), get her off the premises before she had a chance to bite their father.

Mr Green did not help matters by going directly to Nanny Piggins' room and throwing all her designer dresses and circus memorabilia out of the upstairs window and onto the nature strip.

Nanny Piggins and the children soon gathered it all up and packed it away in her travelling trunk.

'Where are you going to go?' asked Samantha.

'Hmm,' said Nanny Piggins. 'I haven't decided yet. But not far. Your father has seriously irritated me today and as a point of pride, I will not allow him to go unpunished.'

'What about us?' sniffed Michael. 'Will we ever see you again?'

Nanny Piggins looked shocked at this horrible thought.

'Of course you will!' she exclaimed. 'I could never leave you three. Not after all the things we have been through together.'

'I've called the police,' yelled Mr Green. 'They'll be here in two minutes. You'd better leave if you don't want to be arrested.'

'Okay, so technically I am going to leave for a little bit,' conceded Nanny Piggins, 'but as Samantha rather graphically put it, I shall be like the blood sloshing about inside the atrium of your heart. I'll always be with you in spirit.'

With that Nanny Piggins picked up the handle of her trunk and started dragging it down the street.

Derrick, Samantha and Michael were all crying now. The atriums and ventricles of their hearts were feeling very heavy indeed as they trudged back into their house. It seemed a very sad and drab building without Nanny Piggins' enormous personality to brighten it.

Understandably the children did not sleep well that night. They had enormous faith in their nanny. But in the middle of the night, when you are tired and it's dark, it's hard to think rationally, so they were all thinking dreadful thoughts about never seeing their nanny again.

The next morning when they went down to

breakfast, their spirits sank even lower. There were no pancakes, cakes, éclairs or danishes to greet them. Their father had made himself a bowl of his horrible high-fibre muesli and not prepared anything for them. They were just about to go into the kitchen to see if they could find any cake Nanny Piggins may have left behind (she often hid cake under the floorboards in case of emergencies), but just as they started to rip up the linoleum, their father scraped back his chair.

'Come along,' he ordered. 'I'm driving you to school.'

'You are?' asked Derrick.

Their father had never driven them to school before. Not even the time Samantha had a broken leg and it rained, and the water had dissolved her plaster cast.

'I'm not letting that pig try to make contact with you on the way to school,' said Mr Green. 'I'm one step ahead of her. She can't beat me with her tricky games. I'm a lawyer, I'm smarter than her.'

'I don't think you are,' said Samantha truthfully. The children knew it was terribly hard to pass law exams, but their father could be so dimwitted in so many ways, they always assumed that he had bribed his professors to pass him, or something equally devious.

Fortunately for Samantha, her father was not listening to her (after all she was only the girl-child), he was too busy ushering them out onto the street.

'But Father, I'm hungry,' protested Michael.

'And we don't have our schoolbags,' protested Derrick.

'Stop whining,' ordered Mr Green as he busily triple-locked the front door. (He'd had a locksmith around the previous evening, trying to pig-proof the house, so he did not notice that his children had stopped complaining.)

They were too busy staring at the beautiful red and gold gypsy caravan parked on the street. It had big wagon wheels, two little shuttered windows, an arching roof, window boxes filled with flowers and lots and lots of decorative trim.

When their father finally turned round he flinched in horror. 'What is that monstrosity?'

'It looks like a gypsy caravan,' said Samantha.

'Gypsies!' panicked Mr Green. He'd had a rational fear of gypsies ever since a Gypsy Queen had kidnapped him and tried to force him to marry her. (For more information, see Chapter 12 of *Nanny Piggins and the Wicked Plan*.)

Just then the little shuttered windows of the caravan flew open and Nanny Piggins popped her head out. 'Yoo-hoo!' she called. 'Would you like a slice of cake before you go to school?'

The children rushed forward, partly to grab a slice of cake but mainly to hug their beloved ex-nanny.

'What is the meaning of this?' demanded Mr Green. 'This is an outrage!' His mouth continued to open and close while he tried to think of more coherent things to say. 'I won't stand for it . . . This is unacceptable . . . I'm calling the police.'

'No need,' said Nanny Piggins happily. 'The Police Sergeant is here already.'

The other little shuttered window of the caravan swung open and the Police Sergeant popped his head out. 'Good morning, Mr Green,' he called, before taking another bite of his shortbread cookie.

'I demand that you remove this pig from my premises!' yelled Mr Green.

'She isn't on your premises,' said the Police Sergeant. 'She's parked her caravan on a public street, as she is fully within her rights to do. There are no legal grounds on which I could remove her.'

'Another shortbread cookie, Sergeant?' asked Nanny Piggins.

'Don't mind if I do,' said the Sergeant. (He was normally a very honest man, who would never dream of taking anything that could be misconstrued as a bribe. But he did have a weakness for shortbread cookies, a fact Nanny Piggins knew full well.)

'I'll go over your head,' spluttered Mr Green. 'I'll go to the Chief Superintendent.'

'You can, but the laws which protect the rights of travelling people are very old ones,' said the Police Sergeant. 'The Chief Superintendent may be sympathetic to your cause, but the law is the law. You should know. Didn't they teach you that at law school?'

Mr Green went red and then purple in the face as he tried and failed to think of something cutting to say.

'You'd better move along, Mr Green,' advised the Police Sergeant, 'before one of the neighbours calls me complaining about the amount of noise you are making so early in the morning.'

Mr Green stomped off, taking the children with him (but not before Nanny Piggins had handed them each a packed lunch of chocolate, cake and chocolate cake so they would not starve under their father's care).

'I think that's round one to Nanny Piggins,' whispered Derrick to Samantha and Michael as they slid into the back of their father's Rolls-Royce.

When the children came home from school that afternoon they were disappointed to discover that, while the gypsy caravan was still parked in the street, there was no-one inside.

'You don't suppose Father's found some way to chase her off, do you?' asked Michael.

'I can't imagine how he could,' said Derrick, 'short of buying a tank.'

When they let themselves into the house, their spirits were low. That was until the wallpaper started talking to them.

'Did you have a good day at school?' asked the wallpaper.

'What?' asked Derrick. He had never been spoken to by an interior decoration before.

'It's okay,' said the wallpaper. 'It's me!' The wallpaper now moved. It seemed to wave at them. Then they all realised it was Nanny Piggins. She was entirely covered in body paint so that she looked exactly like the ugly forty-year-old floral wallpaper that lined their house.

'Nanny Piggins!' exclaimed Samantha, rushing forward to hug her.

'Freeze!' yelled Nanny Piggins. 'You mustn't hug me. Your father is watching with his video cameras.'

'What video cameras?' asked Michael.

'Up there,' said Nanny Piggins, gesturing to a camera attached to the ceiling. 'He's had them installed in every room so he can watch you all the time. But fortunately for us, he did not bother paying the extra to have microphones installed, so we can say whatever we like and he can't hear us.'

'Good,' said Derrick, turning to scowl at the camera, 'because I want to say that our father is the biggest . . .'

Unfortunately Derrick never got to share his thoughts because at that moment an incredibly loud voice barked out around the house.

'DON'T STAND AROUND DILLY-DALLYING. I WANT TO SEE YOU ALL DOING YOUR HOMEWORK, RIGHT NOW! QUICK STICKS!' boomed the voice.

'What on earth was that?' asked Michael.

'I forgot to mention,' explained Nanny Piggins. 'Your father has had speakers installed in every room so that he can broadcast instructions to you.'

'So he can speak to us but we can't speak to him?' asked Samantha.

'Yes, he does seem to have engineered this whole scenario to suit himself,' agreed Nanny Piggins.

Once they got used to the new arrangements,

Nanny Piggins and the children found they could be easily worked around. All it took was a dollop of whipped cream smeared over the lenses of the cameras at crucial moments, then they could all jump out the window and run off down the street. So in reality all that high-tech monitoring equipment barely altered their routine.

One day, when the children got off their school bus in the afternoon, they found Nanny Piggins waiting for them.

'Why aren't you wearing your body paint?' asked Samantha. 'Aren't you going to spend the afternoon with us?'

'Of course I am,' said Nanny Piggins, 'but this morning I had an even better idea about how to thwart your father.'

'What is it?' asked Michael.

'I've painted life-size cardboard cut-outs of each of you and positioned them in front of the cameras in your house,' explained Nanny Piggins, 'so right now it looks like you are sitting quietly in the living room doing maths.'

'But won't Father be suspicious if we never move?' asked Samantha.

'No, it would be his dream come true,' said Derrick.

'So what are we going to do now?' asked Michael.

'Well, you are probably dangerously weak after having to endure an entire day at school,' said Nanny Piggins, 'so I suggest we start by going to the ice-cream shop and having a giant banana split, without the bananas of course.'

And that is exactly what they did. In fact they ended up spending the whole afternoon at the ice-cream parlour. Nanny Piggins convinced Andre the owner to allow her to use the ice-cream to create a life-sized sculpture of Mr Green. It was a very convincing depiction. She used strawberry ice-cream for his head and hands, chocolate icing for his hair and eyebrows, and pistachio and hazelnut ice-cream for his grey–green suit. The statue was so convincing it made Samantha shudder and feel guilty about not doing her homework every time she looked at it. And it turned out to be quite a boon for the ice-cream shop because Nanny Piggins invited all the other patrons to throw glacé cherries at Mr Green's head, something they all enjoyed enormously. Before they left, Andre made Nanny Piggins promise to come back the following week and do another statue of someone unpleasant, perhaps Headmaster Pimple-stock, to shock and appal his patrons.

So it was eight o'clock at night when Nanny Piggins walked the children home, laughing and talking about their wonderful evening. But when they arrived at their front gate they were greeted by an unhappy sight. Mr Green was standing on the front doorstep waiting for them. And he looked very cross.

'What are you doing here?' demanded Nanny Piggins. 'You usually aren't home for hours yet.'

'It's my house!' yelled Mr Green. 'I'll come home when I like! You are fired! You should not be going anywhere near my children!'

'It's not my fault I bumped into them coming out of the library and we all happened to be walking the same way along the street,' said Nanny Piggins.

'I don't believe that for one instant,' shrieked Mr Green. 'How do you explain the fact that you all have ice-cream smeared across your hair and clothing?'

'Um . . .' said Derrick.

'Because an ice-cream truck crashed and we stopped to render assistance, of course,' said Nanny Piggins. 'What other explanation could there be?'

Mr Green looked like his head was ready to explode he was so angry, but somehow he managed to rope in his temper. 'I do not have time for this,' he hissed. 'I received a phone call today from the

Department of Child Services. They are sending a social worker around to inspect the children. She will be here in three minutes. I need you all to get in the house this instant, clean off that ice-cream and do your homework.'

'If you were a good father, wouldn't you be feeding them dinner?' asked Nanny Piggins.

'Do your homework, eat dinner, whatever!' exploded Mr Green. 'I want you to get in the house and pretend to be good children right now!'

'Good evening,' said a woman walking along the street.

'Go away,' yelled Mr Green. 'Can't you see I'm in the middle of admonishing an ex-member of my domestic staff?'

'Domestic staff?' said Nanny Piggins. 'I was the only member of your domestic staff.'

'Just get out of here,' yelled Mr Green. 'Go on, get in your caravan and leave my children alone.'

Nanny Piggins sauntered back to her gypsy caravan and slammed the door.

'Good evening,' said the woman again.

'I thought I told you to go away,' yelled Mr Green.

'Yes, I think you might like to rethink your tone,' said the woman, as she reached into her handbag and pulled out her ID badge. 'I'm Agatha Crawford from the Department of Child Services. I've come to inspect your child-care arrangements.'

'Oh,' said Mr Green.

'Several of your neighbours have contacted us with their concerns,' continued Agatha. 'They are all distressed that you've fired your nanny, but we have received conflicting accounts as to how you look after the children now. Mrs Simpson is worried that you are tying them up in the attic, the Retired Army Colonel who lives round the corner is concerned that you will ship them off to join the French Foreign Legion, and Mrs Lau from across the street is upset that you are keeping your children in the basement under house arrest and forcing them to hand-make sneakers.'

'Don't be ridiculous!' spluttered Mr Green.

'Yes,' said Nanny Piggins, sticking her head out of her caravan window. 'He has installed the sewing machines, but he hadn't got around to getting the shoe-making supplies yet.'

'You shut up!' growled Mr Green.

'Perhaps we should go in the house,' suggested the social worker. 'We can't stand out here on the street leaving your children unattended.'

'What?' said Mr Green. 'No, of course not.'

'Would you like me to come too?' asked Nanny Piggins.

'No!' bellowed Mr Green.

As he led the social worker into the house, he did what he always did after an unpleasant show of emotion. He pretended it had never happened. So, with a forced smile, he showed her into the living room, where Derrick, Samantha and Michael were now sitting, immaculately groomed and doing their homework.

'These are my children,' said Mr Green. 'Derrick, Samantha and Mitchell.'

'Michael,' corrected Michael.

'What?' asked Mr Green.

'My name is Michael,' said Michael.

'No, it's not,' said Mr Green. 'I think I know my own son's name.'

'It says Michael on my birth certificate,' said Michael.

'It must be a typo,' said Mr Green. 'You know what secretaries are like.' He chortled. 'All air between their ears.'

'I used to be a secretary,' Agatha informed him.

'Really?' said Mr Green. 'I don't suppose you could make me a cup of tea then?'

'Even secretaries don't make tea anymore,' said Agatha.

'Mine does,' said Mr Green.

'I bet she spits in it,' muttered Derrick.

'So I take it that the well-dressed, ice-cream-smeared pig living in the caravan outside is your former nanny?' asked the social worker, consulting her notes. 'Miss Sarah Matahari Lorelai Piggins?'

'World's Greatest Flying Pig,' added Samantha.

'Nobel Laureate,' added Derrick.

'And master baker,' added Michael.

'And convicted criminal!' added Mr Green.

'What was her crime?' asked Agatha, her pen held at the ready.

'Tightrope walking,' explained Samantha.

'Tightrope walking?' asked Agatha. 'And how did this endanger the children?'

'It didn't,' said Derrick.

'She broke the law!' declared Mr Green. 'She set a bad example.'

'Yes, but you have to understand that I work with the Department of Child Services,' said Agatha. 'I'm used to dealing with people who commit crimes like selling their children, or setting fire to their houses while their children are inside playing with Lego. I've never come across a case of tightrope walking before. Did she do it to get away from the children and neglect her duties?'

'No, she did it to fetch us a slice of chocolate cake,' explained Michael.

'I see,' said Agatha, writing on a large notepad. 'So what alternative child-care arrangements have you made.'

'I've been looking after the children myself,' said Mr Green proudly.

'Really?' said Agatha, looking up. 'Because when I rang Botswana and spoke to your employer earlier today, Ms Isabella Dunkhurst, she said you work 95 hours a week, every week. So how is that possible?'

'I had video cameras installed,' said Mr Green, proudly indicating the video camera on the ceiling of the room.'

'And he yells at us through loudspeakers,' added Derrick.

'And you thought this would substitute for the loving presence of a responsible adult?' asked Agatha.

'Well, it's a darn sight better than having a criminal pig look after them,' said Mr Green.

'No it's not,' corrected Agatha. 'I've received testimonials from everyone living in your street about what a wonderful job Nanny Piggins does looking after your children.'

'Even Mrs McGill, the nasty old lady next door?' asked Derrick.

'Yes, even her,' said the social worker. 'She's impressed by how much outdoor exercise Nanny Piggins makes sure your children get, by running into her backyard and stealing lemons from her tree.'

'Nanny Piggins does not normally approve of fruit,' Samantha explained, 'but she does like a little lemon zest in a victoria sponge.'

'You can't force me to re-hire her,' spluttered Mr Green.

'Yes I can,' said the social worker. 'It's either that or I charge you with child neglect. Then *you'll* be the one with a criminal record.'

Mr Green went white at the horrible thought. 'But everyone at work would laugh at me.'

'When are you going to realise, Father,' asked Samantha kindly, 'that they are always going to laugh at you?'

'I can't do it,' said Mr Green. 'I can't bring myself to do it.'

'It's because you're frightened of Nanny Piggins, isn't it?' guessed Derrick.

Mr Green nodded and sniffed a little.

Just then Nanny Piggins burst back into the room. 'Don't worry, Mr Green,' declared Nanny Piggins. 'I re-hire myself. Another chore I'll save you from having to do yourself.'

'Thank you,' muttered Mr Green weakly.

'But I'm afraid I do insist on renegotiating my contract,' said Nanny Piggins. 'I want more money.'

'Oh no,' said Mr Green, going white again.

'If I am going to return, I insist on being paid . . . eleven cents an hour!' declared Nanny Piggins boldly.

'It's a deal!' exclaimed Mr Green with relief. He knew a good deal when he heard one. 'Can I go back to my office now.' He looked from Nanny Piggins to the social worker for their permission. They both nodded and he ran out of the house.

'What a dreadful man,' said the social worker.

'In his defence,' said Nanny Piggins, 'he usually behaves himself very well. Sometimes we can go weeks without noticing he lives here.'

The children nodded.

'Well, this calls for a celebration!' said Nanny Piggins. 'Michael, run along the street and invite all the neighbours over for a party. I'm going to replicate the cake that caused all this trouble – the one I tightrope-walked between buildings for.'

'You're going to throw a neighbourhood party on a school night?' scowled the social worker.

'Don't worry,' said Nanny Piggins. 'You're invited too. In fact, you're the guest of honour.'

'That means you get the largest slice of cake,' Samantha told her.

The social worker was soon charmed by Nanny Piggins' homemade baked goods, and they all had a wonderful party with delicious cake and a tightrope-walk re-enactment that the neighbours talked about for years to come.

Even Mr Green had a lovely time, at his office, fudging his clients' tax returns into the small hours of the morning.

CHAPTER 9

Nanny Piggins and the Art of Advice

When Derrick, Samantha and Michael emerged from school they were surprised to see their father's Rolls-Royce sitting outside the gates with the engine running. They were surprised for two reasons. First, in the entire time they had been at school they had never, not once, been picked up by their father. (Not even the day their mother had gone missing in that mysterious boating accident. Even then he let them catch the bus home before breaking the terrible news.) Second, the street outside the school gates was a 'No standing' zone, and Mr Green would never have the courage to disobey a sign put up by the municipal council.

'Is that Father's car?' asked Samantha in bewilderment.

'Who else do we know who owns a vomit-yellow Rolls-Royce?' asked Michael.

'It must be Nanny Piggins,' said Samantha. 'She must have "borrowed" it.'

'But Father had all the locks changed and only one key pressed, which he keeps hidden on a chain around his neck,' said Derrick.

'I knew that sounded like a bad idea as soon as I heard it,' said Michael. 'As if Nanny Piggins would let a little thing like Father's neck stand between her and the Rolls-Royce.'

As the children approached the car, a tinted window rolled down and they could see a figure entirely dressed in black and wearing a balaclava, sitting behind the wheel.

'Eeek!' said Samantha. 'It's a car thief!'

'If it was a car thief, why would they come and pick us up from school?' reasoned Michael.

'Perhaps they feel bad about being a car thief,' suggested Samantha.

Just then the black clad figured pulled up her balaclava, revealing herself to be none other than their beloved nanny.

'Quick, get in!' called Nanny Piggins.

'How on earth did you get hold of Father's car?' asked Derrick.

'You didn't cut his head off, did you?' asked Michael, although he doubted if she did it would do their father much harm. Chickens can survive for weeks with their heads cut off, provided you keep putting food down their oesophagi. And his father often reminded him of a chicken.

'No no, not at all,' said Nanny Piggins. 'I didn't have the time. I just borrowed a half brick from Mrs Simpson and dropped it in through the sunroof.'

The children peered into the car to see the gaping hole.

'He should thank me really,' said Nanny Piggins. 'Convertibles are much more fashionable and he could do with some work on his tan.'

The children were not entirely sure their father would see it that way.

'Hurry up and get in,' urged Nanny Piggins. 'We've got work to do. I've got balaclavas for all of you so the police won't be able to prove anything.'

The children obediently got in the car and pulled their balaclavas over their faces, as Nanny Piggins peeled away, with tyres squealing.

'Where are we going?' asked Derrick.

'To teach someone a lesson,' explained Nanny Piggins.

'Who?' worried Samantha.

'The advice columnist from the newspaper. She's been at it again,' said Nanny Piggins. 'See for yourselves.' Nanny Piggins passed a copy of the local newspaper back to the children.

They scanned it quickly. It seemed like pretty standard sort of advice. 'Be honest with your husband.' 'Save ten per cent of your income.' 'Buy your wife some flowers once in a while.'

'Which one are we meant to be shocked by?' asked Derrick.

'The second one from the bottom!' said Nanny Piggins.

Michael read it aloud: '*Dear Aunt Alice, I put on a couple of kilos over Christmas and I just can't lose it again. I've tried three different diets but nothing works. What should I do? Yours, Frumpy*'

'Now read the response,' said Nanny Piggins.

Samantha read: '*Dear Frumpy, Why don't you take up jogging?*'

'Can you believe it?' exclaimed Nanny Piggins. 'Jogging, I mean jogging!'

'What's wrong with jogging?' asked Michael. He had never tried it himself but he wasn't aware that there was anything terribly wrong with it. 'I thought you said people who wanted to lose weight should exercise.'

'But not jogging!' said Nanny Piggins. 'It is the most humiliating and degrading of all sports. It's even worse than beach volleyball. And you have to do that wearing a bikini and sticking your bottom out for everyone to look at.'

'But lots of people jog,' said Derrick. 'Presidents do it.'

'I know,' said Nanny Piggins. 'That's the tragedy. They have no-one in their lives to tell them how stupid they look bouncing up and down. And all that sweating! So disgusting. But that's not the worst thing about jogging.'

'It's not?' asked Samantha. She thought bouncing and sweating sounded pretty bad.

'The worst part is that it's so utterly, miserably boring,' said Nanny Piggins. 'Just pounding along the road, one foot in front of the other, desperately trying not to think about the pain in your legs.'

'But you run all the time,' Derrick pointed out.

'That's different,' said Nanny Piggins. 'I run away from dangerous things like police officers. Or I run towards delicious things like ice-cream vans. That's exciting and purposeful, whereas jogging is just painful and pointless.'

'So what are we going to do about it?' asked Samantha.

'We're going to kidnap Aunt Alice,' declared Nanny Piggins.

'What?' exclaimed all three children.

'Nanny Piggins,' said Derrick. 'You can't!'

'Why not?' asked Nanny Piggins. 'She's had it coming for months now.'

'You can't kidnap her, it's illegal!' said Samantha. 'Seriously illegal. You'll get more than community service if you get caught.'

'Pish!' said Nanny Piggins. 'I've been kidnapped lots of times and I've never come to any harm.'

'Yes, but you're circus folk,' argued Derrick. 'The advice columnist isn't. She won't like it.'

'Oh piffle,' said Nanny Piggins. 'All I'm going to do is throw her in a sack, drive her down to the local jogging track and make her do fifty or sixty laps to see how she likes it.'

Nanny Piggins hit the brakes and the car screeched to a halt.

'Here's where she lives,' said Nanny Piggins. 'Now pass me that sack, rope and gaffer tape.'

'How did you get her address?' asked Samantha. 'I thought the editor had ordered his staff not to give it to you.'

'Hah!' scoffed Nanny Piggins. 'He was easily dealt with. I just baked him one of my quadruple fudge cakes and when he passed out from a calorie high, I rifled through his address book.'

Nanny Piggins took her equipment and bounded out of the car.

'We've got to stop her,' said Derrick.

'How?' asked Samantha. 'She's never listened to reason before.'

'If only we had our own sack, rope and gaffer tape, we could kidnap her,' said Michael.

'She is always urging us to take those things to school,' said Samantha repentantly.

'Come on,' said Derrick, 'we'd better catch up with her. The least we can do is yell "run" when Nanny Piggins kicks in the door.'

But, somewhat to Nanny Piggins' disappointment, she never got to kick in the door. Because before she even pressed the doorbell the door swung open, revealing a nice old lady.

'Hello,' said the old lady. 'Have you come to sell me something? Do come in and tell me all about it.'

'Do you often get four door-to-door salesmen turning up wearing balaclavas?' asked Derrick.

'No,' admitted Aunt Alice, 'but I don't want to second-guess your sales tactic. Now come on in for a cup of tea. I've got some lovely flapjack I baked this morning.'

At the mention of baked goods the steam entirely went out of Nanny Piggins' anger. 'Flapjack? Where?' she asked. 'Never mind. I'll find it,' she shouted as she pushed past Aunt Alice and ran into the house, looking for the kitchen.

They soon found Nanny Piggins chomping her way through half a tray of golden, sticky treats. 'Not bad,' conceded Nanny Piggins. 'But that does not excuse your dreadful behaviour.'

'It doesn't?' asked Aunt Alice. 'What have I done?'

'You've given out simply terrible advice,' accused Nanny Piggins, popping another square of flapjack in her mouth.

'Oh, I know,' said Aunt Alice, helping herself to a square of flapjack too, 'but it's so hard thinking up what to say. I get bored with myself sometimes.'

'But that is a terrible attitude,' accused Nanny Piggins. 'These people turn to you for help. You can't let them down.'

'Oh, don't worry,' said Aunt Alice. 'I don't let *real* people down. You see, I don't just make up the answers, I make up the letters too.'

'I beg your pardon?' exclaimed Nanny Piggins.

'Nobody writes to the newspaper wanting advice anymore,' said Aunt Alice, 'and when they do, the things they ask about are rarely fit for print.'

'They're about exercising?' guessed Nanny Piggins.

'No, it's all about relationships,' said Aunt Alice, 'and I've been single my whole life, so I don't know much about all that sort of stuff. That's why I make up the questions as well as the answers. It's easier that way.'

'That's awful,' denounced Nanny Piggins. 'I'm afraid I'm going to have to get you fired.'

'Not out of a cannon?' queried Michael.

'No, from her job,' said Nanny Piggins.

'Please don't,' said Aunt Alice. 'I rather like having a job and earning money. It helps me to pay for food and such like.'

'Don't worry,' said Nanny Piggins, 'I'm not a cruel pig. I'll make sure you get another job that suits you much better.'

And Nanny Piggins was true to her word. By five o'clock that afternoon she had been to see the editor again, woken him up from his fudge-cake-induced slumber by giving him a slice of coffee cake, and insisted he sack his advice columnist.

The editor was, at first, resistant. Aunt Alice had once given him excellent advice on how to get a blueberry stain out of white woollen carpet, so he was very loyal to her. And since he never read her column (he was a very lazy editor), he did not realise how rotten it had become.

'But she's a sweet old lady,' protested the editor. 'I can't sack her. The union will come after me.'

'I'm not suggesting you leave her penniless on the street,' said Nanny Piggins.

'You're not?' said the editor.

'No, I think you should give her a job she is actually qualified to do,' explained Nanny Piggins. 'Her flapjack is really very good. The best I've ever tasted cooked by a human. So I think you should give her a cooking column.'

'I suppose I could do that,' said the editor, 'but what about the advice column. It's been part of the paper for eighty years. I can't cut that.'

'Don't worry,' said Nanny Piggins. 'I'll write it for you.'

'You?' said the editor.

'Why not me?' said Nanny Piggins.

'You can read and write?' asked the editor.

'Of course I can!' said Nanny Piggins. 'What are you trying to imply.'

'She is actually very good at writing,' said Derrick, chipping in to help his nanny. 'Particularly angry letters and rude letters. She writes those most days.'

Nanny Piggins nodded with agreement. 'And I get into lots and lots of trouble all the time. So I have plenty of advice I could give people.'

'You do?' asked the editor sceptically.

'Yes,' said Nanny Piggins. 'For example, given my current legal predicament, I could now advise anyone wanting to eat a slice of birthday cake not to tightrope walk between two buildings.'

'You would?' asked Samantha, relieved to hear her nanny sounding so sensible.

'Yes, I would advise them to blast themselves from a cannon instead,' said Nanny Piggins. 'The police never would have been able to prove it was me if I was just a blur of speed across the sky.'

Eventually the editor decided he would give Nanny Piggins a go as his new advice columnist. He was sure that whatever she wrote, while not necessarily being good advice, would certainly be entertaining advice. And that's all that mattered to him as a newspaper man. Plus Nanny Piggins bribed him with promises of more fudge cake, so she soon had her way.

Nanny Piggins was looking forward to her first day at work as a professional advice columnist. She had been giving people unsolicited advice for years, free of charge, so it seemed only fair that she now be paid for the service. She had bought herself a typewriter. (She did not like computers because they did not make a loud 'ping' at the end of every line.) And of course she had bought a very large supply of chocolate (the most essential supply for any writer). Now she and the children just had to await the arrival of the first sack of mail asking for advice.

'It's just like waiting for Santa to come,' said Nanny Piggins excitedly, 'only instead of getting a bunch of rubbishy plastic toys, we're getting something really good – lots of sordid stories about people's real lives.'

'I don't think you're meant to enjoy reading

about other people's problems,' said Samantha dubiously.

'Don't be ridiculous,' said Nanny Piggins. 'Of course you are. That's what all forms of entertainment are based on. It's why soap operas are so good. It's wonderful enjoying the misery of others. It makes you forget about your own problems for a while.'

'I can see the postman,' Boris' voice crackled over a walkie-talkie. He was stationed up on top of the roof as lookout.

'How many sacks has he got?' asked Nanny Piggins, speaking into her own walkie-talkie.

'Only one, I think' said Boris. 'It's hard to tell from this distance.'

'Here,' said Nanny Piggins, giving Michael a big slice of the most delicious-looking moist chocolate mud cake. 'Run down the road and take this to the postman. It'll give him the energy to hurry up.'

Nanny Piggins danced excitedly from one trotter to the other. It showed enormous strength of character on her part that she was able to resist the urge to burst out of the house, run down the road and just snatch the sack from the postman. But she knew she should not, because the postman had taken out a restraining order against her. (He had not wanted to but his wife insisted because Nanny Piggins kept leaping out of trees and giving him haircuts. They were fashionable haircuts, but his wife didn't like it when her husband came home looking like a European soccer player. If it weren't for the postal uniform she wouldn't recognise him.)

Finally they heard the thud of a sack being dropped on their doorstep, the knock at the door and the pitter-patter of rapid footsteps as the postman ran away. Nanny Piggins wrenched open the door and looked down, only to be slightly discouraged. There was a sack of mail. But it was a very small sack.

'Is that it?' she asked. 'I thought there'd be a lot more troubled people than that.'

Nanny Piggins, Boris and the children enjoyed their morning reading all the mail. They were, at first, disappointed to discover just how many of the letters were from people complaining that they either could not get a girlfriend, or could not get a boyfriend. These letters were easily dealt with. Nanny Piggins was not going to waste newspaper column space on them. She simply forwarded all the letters from men complaining they couldn't meet women to the women complaining they couldn't meet men, and vice versa, so they could sort their problems out for themselves. But there were other problems that were far more tricky.

'I've got one here from a woman who says, *My husband cuts his toenails in the living room and never picks up the clippings. What should I do?*', read Samantha.

'Ah, that is a good one,' agreed Nanny Piggins. 'Derrick, sit at the typewriter and take this down: *Cut off his cake supply!*'

'That's a bit extreme,' protested Samantha.

'No it isn't,' said Nanny Piggins. 'True, toenail clippings are tiny. But it's what they represent. Any man who does not know that clipping his toenails all over the living room floor is disgusting is inconsiderate in the extreme and should be punished.'

'Father clips his toenails in the living room,' said Michael.

'Exactly,' said Nanny Piggins, nodding her head.

'I've got a good letter here,' said Michael. *'I am the headmaster of a school but no-one has any respect for me anymore. Not since a pig has entered my life. She contradicts everything I say, wrecks school property and embarrasses me constantly. What should I do? Signed Headmaster Put-upon.'*

'Hmm,' said Nanny Piggins. 'I don't think Headmaster Put-upon is his real name. I suspect this letter is secretly from Headmaster Pimplestock.'

'It does seem likely,' agreed Samantha.

'Derrick, take this down,' called Nanny Piggins. *'Dear Headmaster Put-upon, my advice to you is to shut yourself in your office and don't come out. You should be thankful to have a pig as a member of your school community. Pigs are better at just about everything than humans, so stay out of her way and just get on with it.'*

'Listen to this,' said Boris. 'This letter is from a woman who is worried that her identical twin sister is secretly running an arms smuggling business with her husband.'

'Oh that's easy,' said Nanny Piggins. 'The same thing happened to Brianna on *The Young and the Irritable*. All she needs to do is pose as a Columbian cartel chief, kidnap her husband and have their helicopter crash over a deserted tropical island. There, they can fall in love again while fighting off deadly snakes, starvation and her wicked ex-husband, Bridge.'

'Here's another one,' said Samantha. *'Dear Aunt Alice, I've got a white chocolate stain on my white blouse. I can't see it, but I know it is there. How do I get it out? Yours Hygienically, Nanny Anastasia.'*

'You don't suppose that's from Nanny Anne, do you?' wondered Michael.

'Who else would want to get a chocolate stain *out* of their clothes?' reasoned Nanny Piggins. 'I'm forever trying to put chocolate stains in, just so I have a lovely snack later. Take this down, Derrick: *Dear Nanny Anne, for I know that is your real name. If you want to get out a white chocolate stain but can't see it, simply put a milk chocolate stain right next to it, then suck on the whole area. When the milk chocolate is gone, so is the white chocolate.*'

'There's one here from the Retired Army Colonel who lives around the corner,' said Michael. 'He writes, *Dear Aunt Alice, I'm desperately in love with the world's most glamorous flying pig. How can I convince her to marry me?*'

'Oh dear,' said Nanny Piggins. 'This is an awkward situation. Derrick, type this up: *Dear Retired Army Colonel, Some things, like the aurora borealis or volcanic eruptions, are best admired from afar. Why not try dating someone your own age and species?*'

And so Nanny Piggins ploughed her way through the mail bag solving problems. When they finished the last letter they were quite sad.

'Well that was fun,' said Nanny Piggins. 'I always knew humans had terrible problems – you can tell from the ridiculous way they dress – but

I never realised they were so clueless as to how to solve them.'

'You've written pages and pages of material,' said Derrick. 'Now you just have to decide which ones you want published in the newspaper.'

'What do you mean?' asked Nanny Piggins. 'Obviously I want all of them published.'

'But that's not the way it works,' said Samantha. 'The advice column only ever prints five or six letters. You've answered nearly a hundred letters here today. If you printed them all it would take up the whole newspaper.'

'And so it should,' said Nanny Piggins. 'This stuff is much more interesting than that "world news" or "stock market analysis".'

'I don't think the editor will see it that way,' said Michael.

Nanny Piggins rolled her eyes. 'Am I going to have to go down to his office and berate him again? This is really getting wearisome. Come on, if we get the two o'clock bus we'll have an hour or two to spend in the lolly shop first.'

After much yelling and some foot stomping, Nanny Piggins and the editor reached a compromise. While he would not give over his whole newspaper to Nanny Piggins' advice column, he did agree to increase the space he devoted to it tenfold, giving her a double-page spread. (Because after Michael showed him some of her advice, he could not deny that it was much more exciting than anything else in the paper, including the world news, celebrity marriages and stories about baked bean factories exploding from gas leaks.)

The new advice column was an immediate success. Most advice columnists use moderation and carefully toned advice so as not to distress or upset the recipient. Nanny Piggins had no such qualms. She had no money so she did not care if she was sued. And she was a former flying pig, so death threats did not frighten her (when you've been blasted by a cannon, not much scares you). As a result, her column was a gripping read.

The following week a mailman drove up with a truck and unloaded three tonnes of mail all over their front yard.

'How wonderful,' said Nanny Piggins delight-edly. 'I told you the humans in this town were deeply troubled. I'm glad they've found time to write to me about it.'

So once again Nanny Piggins set to work solving problems. By the end of the third week on the job, you could see the effect of her work about town.

People were smiling more. Single men had found single women and were holding hands in the street. The headmaster had not left his office in a fortnight and the school was running much more smoothly. And Hans' bakery was doing a roaring trade, since Nanny Piggins was telling so many people they could solve their problems if they just ate more cake. The Lord Mayor himself had called to thank Nanny Piggins. He had been trying to lose weight for twenty years, and now he'd lost ten kilos, all because his toenail clippings had triggered such a dramatic change in his wife's cooking.

Everything was going very well until one day when Nanny Piggins and the children stepped out the front door and suddenly they were attacked, scooped up in a giant sack, and dumped in the back of a truck.

'What's going on?' shrieked Samantha.

'Don't panic,' said Nanny Piggins. 'We're just being kidnapped.'

'Kidnapped?!' exclaimed Derrick.

'Yes,' said Nanny Piggins. 'It's probably the Ringmaster, wanting me to come down to the circus and solve all his problems. Stuffing people in sacks is just his way of saying hello.'

'But what if we're not being kidnapped by one of

your ex-work colleagues,' panicked Samantha, 'and we're being kidnapped by a sociopathic lunatic.'

'I shouldn't think it will make much difference,' said Nanny Piggins.

Twenty minutes later Nanny Piggins and the children found themselves tied to chairs in a dark basement and confronted by their kidnapper. When she stepped into a shaft of light, they were shocked to see who it was.

'It's Miss Britches!' exclaimed Derrick.

'The Truancy Officer!' exclaimed Samantha.

'Ah yes, another one of my arch-nemeses,' said Nanny Piggins. 'I've got quite a few these days.'

'Silence!' yelled Miss Britches.

'Oooh, here we go, it's starting,' said Nanny Piggins. 'If you're going to start berating us, could we please have a slice of cake first. It's just that I'm feeling a bit peckish.'

'There will be no cake!' declared Miss Britches.

'She's going to torture us!' exclaimed Nanny Piggins. 'That's not very nice. What did I do? Turn up at a function wearing the same dress as you and make you pale in comparison? Or did I make you a cake so delicious you have never been able to enjoy another slice of cake since? I've ruined so many lives that way.'

'You ruined my life with your terrible advice!' declared Miss Britches.

'Hang about,' said Nanny Piggins. 'That can't be right. I only give brilliant advice, perfectly crafted to improve the life of the troubled recipient every time.'

'Oh yes, you help *them*,' said Miss Britches, 'but have you ever thought how that advice affects the people around them?'

Nanny Piggins paused and considered this for a moment. 'No, I'm afraid I haven't,' she admitted. 'I just assumed that making people's lives better would benefit the rest of society.'

'Well, it hasn't benefitted me!' cried Miss Britches.

'Okay,' said Nanny Piggins. 'First of all, how about we start using our inside voices? Remember, I'm not a human, I'm a pig, so my hearing is twenty times better than yours, which means there is absolutely no reason to yell – unless I'm eating cake and you need to make yourself heard above my moans of delight.'

'All right,' agreed Miss Britches petulantly.

'And second,' continued Nanny Piggins, 'why don't you explain exactly what I've done. All this intrigue is very thrilling. But it is also very time consuming – time that could be much better spent eating cake.'

Miss Britches took a deep breath and started speaking at a normal volume. 'My boyfriend wrote to you,' she began to explain.

'He's not the one I told to take up trainspotting, is he?' asked Nanny Piggins. 'Because I can understand why you would find that upsetting.'

'No. You told my boyfriend to dump me!' said Miss Britches.

'Oh,' said Nanny Piggins. 'Why did I do that?'

'You said that I was clearly a narcissistic maniac with anger management problems,' accused Miss Britches.

'You got that bit right,' muttered Michael.

'Hey!' yelled Miss Britches.

'All right, calm down,' said Nanny Piggins. 'But surely you're better off without some weak-willed boyfriend who takes advice from a newspaper column. He's clearly a twit. If you like I can write him another letter and get him to take you back.'

'But that's not all,' said Miss Britches. 'My boss at social services wrote to you too.'

'I don't like the way this is going,' said Derrick.

'What did I tell him?' asked Nanny Piggins.

'To fire me,' yelled Miss Britches. 'You said my terrible temper was scaring my co-workers.'

'Is that all?' asked Nanny Piggins. 'Well I'm sure we can find you another job.'

'It is not all!' cried Miss Britches. 'You also told the man at my local bakery to cut me off, saying that such an angry customer did not deserve cake; you told my dry-cleaner to join the army; you told my landlord to evict me and my next door neighbour to climb over the fence and steal my clothes pegs.'

'Oh dear,' said Nanny Piggins.

'Everyone I know has written to you for advice,' accused Miss Britches, 'and you have advised every single one of them to either leave me or punish me.'

'Yes, there does seem to be a bit of a recurring theme,' agreed Nanny Piggins. 'What an unfortunate coincidence.'

'It's not a coincidence,' shrieked Miss Britches. 'You're systematically ruining my life.'

'That's one way of looking at it,' said Michael. 'The other way of looking at it is that you've systematically ruined your own life by being such a meanie.'

'How dare you!' yelled Miss Britches.

'Ah Michael, we are not here to judge,' chided Nanny Piggins. 'We must be impartial. This poor woman may have been reduced to being a shrieking banshee because everyone else in the world has been mean. Don't worry, I'm sure we can solve your problems.'

'You can?' asked Miss Britches.

'Isn't that what you kidnapped me hoping I could do?' asked Nanny Piggins.

'No, I was going to force you to make a video admitting that you were a fraud – one that I could distribute to all the news networks,' explained Miss Britches.

'That's quite a good idea,' said Nanny Piggins. 'You've got a talent for this. Perhaps we can do that later. But first, let's deal with all these problems of yours.'

'All right,' conceded Miss Britches. 'Where do we start? Are you going to help me kidnap back my boyfriend?'

'No,' admitted Nanny Piggins. 'I suspect the poor man has suffered enough already. No, I think we should start by eating a slice of cake. I think your blood sugar is a little low and it's making you cranky.'

Upstairs in Miss Britches' kitchen Nanny Piggins quickly whipped up a delicious fluffy chocolate cake, which served its purpose. It made Miss Britches stop yelling and threatening Nanny Piggins long enough for her to go out into the hall and make a phone call.

'Who are you calling?' asked Miss Britches between mouthfuls.

'Don't worry about that,' said Nanny Piggins. 'Have another slice of cake. I'm just going to arrange a lovely surprise for you.'

Thirty minutes later, as they were just eating their way through their fourth cake (Miss Britches was very hungry for cake having been cut off by Hans for over a week now), suddenly the kitchen window was smashed in by a flying canister. The canister hit the floor and smoke began to spew out of it.

'Quick, children!' urged Nanny Piggins. 'Hold a slice of cake over your mouths and noses.'

The children had been well trained and immediately did as they were told, because they knew that chocolate cake was an excellent improvised gas mask. Unfortunately Miss Britches was not as trusting of Nanny Piggins' advice and she almost immediately collapsed in a deep sleep onto the floor.

The next moment a short fat-bottomed figure, dressed in a bright red tail coat and wearing a gas mask, came swinging in through the window.

'The Ringmaster!' exclaimed the children from behind their cakey gas masks.

'Sarah Piggins, darling!' exclaimed the Ringmaster. 'It's so good to see you!'

He then kissed her on each cheek (which is not easy when you are wearing a gas mask) and she responded in the traditional way by stomping on each of his feet (which is quite easy when you are holding a slice of cake to your face).

'Is this my latest recruit?' asked the Ringmaster, pointing to Miss Britches slumped on the floor.

'Yes,' said Nanny Piggins. 'She's a remarkable woman. She has quite a talent for the sheer volume with which she can yell, and she's utterly unpleasant. So I'm sure there's no end of ways you'll be able to put her to work at the circus. Either in the freak show or as a barker, shouting out to the crowds.'

'Or both!' suggested the Ringmaster.

'And given her aptitude for kidnapping,' said Nanny Piggins, 'you might even consider putting her on an apprenticeship training program, because really, she's so unpleasant she's got all the skills to make an excellent Ringmaster some day.'

'What a good idea!' exclaimed the Ringmaster. 'It would be good to have a protégé, just in case I accidentally end up having to spend a little time in jail again.'

And so the Ringmaster took Miss Britches away, and Nanny Piggins declared that was the last person she would ever give advice to. She quit her job as advice columnist immediately. The editor was devastated. 'You can't leave!' he exclaimed. 'Circulation has tripled since you started solving everyone's problems.'

'But that's just it,' said Nanny Piggins. 'I shouldn't do that. It's upsetting the balance of nature. Humans are meant to have problems. It's how the world works. You can't all be as remarkable as pigs.'

'But who am I going to get to give advice now?' asked the editor.

'I've got just the woman for you,' said Nanny Piggins. 'Her name is Nanny Anne. You may have heard of her? She loves giving people advice. It is almost always wrong. And some of her ideas about hygiene are dangerously puritanical. But I think getting advice from a hygiene-obsessed lunatic will be enormously entertaining for your readers.'

And so everything returned to normal. The people of Dulsford went back to being just as troubled as they ever were. And Nanny Anne's advice (usually to soak whatever person, thing or body part was causing the problem in disinfectant) helped not at all.

Then one morning Nanny Piggins got a letter from the Ringmaster . . .

Dear Sarah Piggins,
Thank you for sending me Mirabella [for that was Miss Britches' name]. *She has turned out to be such a treasure. She yells so loudly people in the next city know when the freak show is about to start, she frightens away anyone who thinks about complaining that the carnival games are rigged (which of course they all are), and I've put her in charge of the payroll. She intimidated the whole staff so much, not one person complained last week when I paid them in gravel instead of actual money. In short, she is a joy to have around. If I weren't already married to my arch-nemesis, that sociopathic lunatic Madame Savage, I would seriously consider asking Mirabella to marry me.*
Thank you again, your dear friend,
The Ringmaster

'Are you sure you've made the right decision in quitting the column?' asked Samantha. 'You're clearly incredibly talented at solving other people's problems.'

'True, I do have a gift for advice,' agreed Nanny Piggins. 'But as you know I am not a modest pig, and I like to think I'm even better at being a nanny.'

The children could not agree more, and to show their agreement they gave Nanny Piggins a big hug.

Chapter 10

Nanny Piggins and the Bitter End

The children knew things were doomed to go horribly wrong as soon as they heard the probation officer allocate Nanny Piggins her next job. He was sending her to help out at the library. Nanny Piggins and libraries did not rub along well together. Now, do not get me wrong, Nanny Piggins loved books. She was an avid reader, especially at three o'clock in the morning when she should be asleep, or during parent teacher interviews when she was supposed to be listening to long and boring lectures from Head-master Pimplestock. But Nanny Piggins did not care for institutions in general and libraries, in particular, irked her.

You see, all institutions have rules. Lots and lots of rules. And this makes sense if you are running an important institution like a prison – to have rules like 'No letting the murderers escape' is quite wise. Or if you run a hospital, having rules like 'No leaving your car keys inside a patient's chest while perform-ing open heart surgery' is only reasonable. But you do not often get life-threatening situations in a library (unless you get a very nasty infection from a paper cut). So the sheer weight of rules in their local library drove Nanny Piggins to distraction.

Why must she whisper? Would the world really come to an end if she folded over the corner of a page to mark her place? And was it really necessary to fine her just for enjoying a book so much that she did not want to return it for another week? (Or, more realistically, because she had dropped it in a bowl of cake batter and did not want to return it for another week until she had a chance to lick it all off?)

So it was with these dark thoughts in mind that Nanny Piggins reported to work at her local library.

She was already well known to the head librarian. Indeed, Nanny Piggins' picture was stapled to the wall above the lending desk, with the words 'THIS PIG IS BANNED FROM THE LIBRARY' written in bold print underneath.

The children came with Nanny Piggins. They were beginning to worry that their nanny had been caught up in the classic criminal trap of recidivism. Even though she had been doing community service for several months, the number of hours she had to complete had actually increased, not decreased, because she kept getting in trouble with whoever she was sent to help. (People who run community service programs are not always the broadest-minded individuals. They like rules and punishment too much for that.)

'Now remember, Nanny Piggins, no biting,' coached Samantha as they approached the library.

'Yes, don't bite any librarians or any cake,' warned Michael. He knew that librarians were almost as incensed by finding cake crumbs in a first edition as they were about needing stitches in their shins.

'Yes, yes,' muttered Nanny Piggins. 'You know I do try to be good. It's not my fault if these people provoke me.'

'Yes, *we* understand,' said Derrick. 'It's just that

ordinary people, like on a jury, might not understand how "asking you not to sing light opera in the encyclopaedia section" could be seen as provocation for physical violence.'

'It's the way librarians ask you to not do things,' said Nanny Piggins, 'with their reasonable voices and measured smiles. They could be complimenting me on my dress and I'd still want to pinch them.'

'Yes, well at the very least, try not to mention that when you see the head librarian,' said Samantha.

'All right,' grumbled Nanny Piggins. 'I promise not to speak the truth or give unsolicited fashion tips, no matter how desperately she needs them.'

The automatic doors of the library hissed open (the noisiest thing in the library on most days). Nanny Piggins and the children entered. The head librarian was standing behind the lending desk, waiting for them. She glared at Nanny Piggins and Nanny Piggins glared back. They were like gun-fighters facing off at high noon.

'Good morning, Nanny Piggins,' said the head librarian in her quiet and reasonable voice.

Nanny Piggins fought the urge to lunge forward and bite her old nemesis (yet another one). 'Good morning, head librarian,' she said.

'I understand you are here to help us today,' said the librarian.

'That is my court-appointed task, yes,' said Nanny Piggins.

'Well I'm sure we can find plenty to keep you busy,' said the head librarian.

Nanny Piggins moved to enter into the library proper.

'If,' said the head librarian, stopping Nanny Piggins in her tracks, 'you promise not to eat, bake or throw cake; bite, wrestle or berate any library visitors; and you do not, under any circumstances, fold over the corner of a page to mark your place.'

Nanny Piggins trembled as she struggled to control her emotions. She knew she should not argue but she could not help herself. 'What if I discover a bomb in the library?' asked Nanny Piggins, 'and I find a book on bomb disarmament, read it and need to mark the page with the relevant information so I can diffuse the bomb?'

'Then you should write down the page number on a notepad,' said the librarian.

'I don't have a notepad,' said Nanny Piggins.

'Then memorise it,' said the librarian.

'I can't,' said Nanny Piggins. 'Have you ever heard of someone having a photographic memory?

Well I have the opposite of a photographic memory when it comes to numbers. Anything that is even vaguely associated with mathematics makes my mind go blank.'

'If there was a bomb in the library, *and* the only way for you to disarm it was by folding over the corner of a page in the Swahili to Tibetan dictionary, *and* it was the only book in the entire library that has never been borrowed or referred to, I would still want you to walk away, leaving the page unfolded and allowing the entire library to explode,' said the librarian.

'That doesn't make any sense,' said Nanny Piggins.

'It makes complete sense,' said the librarian. 'I know you, Nanny Piggins. I know the chances of the library being blown up by a bomb are very low to nil. Whereas the chances of you *thinking* the library is about to be blown up are probably quite high, which is why we have these rules. Rules that must be obeyed.'

The head librarian and Nanny Piggins glared at each other some more. Nanny Piggins would dearly have loved to give the librarian a good piece of her mind and a good bite on her shin, but she was beginning to feel the pressure of having 5372 hours of community service to work down.

'All right, I agree to your terms,' said Nanny Piggins. 'What do you want me to do to help? Bake a tart, or juggle some books, or get blasted out of something? I'm good at those things.'

'No, thank you,' said the librarian. 'I think we'll take baby steps at first. I'd like you to begin by dusting.'

'Dusting what?' asked Nanny Piggins suspiciously. 'Dusting off my tap shoes and putting on a show?'

'No, I'd like you to begin by dusting the books. All of them,' said the head librarian as she reached under the desk and took out a feather duster.

Nanny Piggins was appalled. 'Is that a dead bird tied to a stick?' She had never seen a duster before because she did not believe in doing housework. Nanny Piggins found if you left dirt and dust long enough it would get swept away eventually when you let the bath overflow, or when your brother the ballet-dancing bear fell through the ceiling in the middle of a torrential rainstorm.

'It's a feather duster,' whispered Samantha. 'People use it to brush the dust off things.'

Nanny Piggins peered at the device. 'So the bird is dead, isn't it?'

'It's just the feathers. There's no bird,' explained Derrick.

'There had to be a bird at some stage,' said Nanny Piggins. 'If I agree to this cleaning, am I going to find some poor naked bird down the back of the reference section?'

'Just get on with it,' said the head librarian, actually beginning to show some mild signs of anger. 'I haven't got time for this, I've got fines to post.'

And so Nanny Piggins kissed the children goodbye, assured them she would get into no trouble (which she honestly believed was true) and set to work serving the community. And to give her credit she dusted admirably for an entire forty-three minutes before she snapped.

She was just brushing off the cobwebs on the eighteenth-century poetry section when children's story time began. Nanny Piggins did not mean to eavesdrop but children's story time is the only occasion when anyone is allowed to speak in a normal voice in the library, so the sound of the junior librarian reading to the children carried over to where she was working.

Nanny Piggins did not realise what the noise was at first because the drone was so deadpan and uninteresting. Even though the librarian was reading about wicked pirates, Nanny Piggins found the sound of her voice was so boring it lulled her to sleep. It was only when she slumped forward and her snout banged on a bookend that Nanny Piggins realised what was going on.

'Oh my goodness!' exclaimed Nanny Piggins. 'The junior librarian is trying to bore the preschool children to death! It's up to me to rescue them!'

Nanny Piggins leapt into action. She vaulted over the picture book rack, snatched the book from the junior librarian and woke up the sleeping children. Then she gave the youngsters a valuable life lesson, by demonstrating exactly how a real pirate would tie up a librarian and throw her overboard. (Nanny Piggins did not really throw the junior librarian into the sea, just over a low set of shelves into the political history section.)

She then proceeded to read the story the way it should be read, acting out all the good bits, paying special attention to the sword fights, the plundering and the swinging from the sails. (There were no sails in the library but Nanny Piggins found that the curtains would do.) After she'd finished reading out the good bits she started to make up even better bits involving crocodiles, an evil helicopter and chipmunks with super-strength.

The head librarian was hard at work in her office issuing fines when she first realised something was dreadfully wrong. She could hear screams of delight coming from the children's corner. *Captain Pugwash* had never made children scream before (except for that one child who was afraid of beards).

When the head librarian marched out into the library it was to find Nanny Piggins hiding behind a bookcase yelling, 'You'll never catch me, ye scurvy dogs!' as the children pelted her with paperbacks.

'What is going on here?' demanded the head librarian.

'I'm helping them appreciate literature,' explained Nanny Piggins.

'The children are throwing books,' accused the head librarian.

'Don't worry, they're only paperbacks,' said Nanny Piggins. 'They won't hurt me.'

'I'm more worried about the books,' said the head librarian.

'But you wanted them dusted,' said Nanny Piggins, 'and throwing them about like this is much better than brushing them with a dead bird.'

'I am calling your probation officer!' announced the head librarian.

And so that is how Nanny Piggins came to find herself sitting once more outside Judge Birchmore's courtroom, waiting to face the magistrate.

'This is so unfair,' moaned Nanny Piggins. 'If I end up going to jail because I dented a few paperbacks, I'll be really cross.'

'Maybe Judge Birchmore will be in a good mood today,' said Samantha optimistically.

The others turned and looked at her.

'Do you really think that's possible?' asked Nanny Piggins.

Samantha burst into tears. 'No,' she sobbed. 'I think she's going to be nasty and cross and send you to jail for a very long time.'

'There, there,' said Nanny Piggins, giving Samantha a hug. 'It will be all right. I'm good friends with so many of the inmates down at the maximum security prison, they'll help me dig my escape tunnel and I'll be home before you know it.'

'But that's the men's maximum security prison,' said Derrick. 'You won't be going there. You'll be going to the women's prison.'

'They have gender-segregated prisons?' exclaimed Nanny Piggins. 'That must make it very difficult doing seating arrangements for their dinner parties.'

'I don't think they allow dinner parties in prison,' said Derrick.

Nanny Piggins shuddered. 'I know they are meant to be horrible places because that is the punishment, but no dinner parties? That's just cruel. And what do they do at the women's prison when the women need someone to reach something off a very high shelf, or open a difficult jam jar?'

'I don't know,' admitted Derrick.

'Perhaps they have a bear there,' guessed Michael. 'Boris always does those things for you.'

'True,' conceded Nanny Piggins. 'I don't know how we ever managed without him. It is so handy having a ten-foot-tall bear around the house. Speaking of which, where is Boris?'

But the children never got to answer.

'The people versus Piggins,' called the bailiff.

'Hello Henry,' replied Nanny Piggins. 'We're over here.'

'Hello Nanny Piggins,' called Henry the bailiff. He and Nanny Piggins had become firm friends during her last visit. Being bitten hard on the shins and then receiving an apology sticky date pudding tends to bond people together. 'Are you going to be a good girl today?'

'I doubt it,' said Nanny Piggins. 'I never leave

the house intending to get in a wrestling match with a man in uniform, and yet it so frequently seems to happen.'

'Well, if it comes to that, just try not to hurt me too much,' said the bailiff. 'It's my anniversary tonight and my wife wants me to take her dancing.'

'All right,' agreed Nanny Piggins. 'I won't aim for your legs. I'll aim for your head. Your wife will never notice a mild concussion.'

'You're probably right,' agreed the bailiff as he led Nanny Piggins into the courtroom.

'Isn't the law firm sending someone to defend you?' asked Michael, scanning the crowd for Montgomery St John.

'Isabella Dunkhurst is still in Botswana,' said Nanny Piggins. 'Every time she tries to leave, they give her more diamonds to stay. And Montgomery St John got fired.'

'What for?' asked Samantha.

'Well, apparently he never did have any chapstick in his car,' explained Nanny Piggins, 'and he's been using that excuse for years. But the receptionist at the firm assured me they'd send a lawyer.'

'They have,' said a surly voice behind them.

Nanny Piggins and the children spun around to see none other than Mr Green.

'Father!' exclaimed the children.

'I'm doomed!' exclaimed Nanny Piggins.

'They've sent me to defend you because I am most familiar with your case,' said Mr Green gloomily.

'But are you even qualified to be a trial lawyer?' asked Derrick.

'It's just a magistrate's hearing,' said Mr Green. 'Anyone can do that. I did go to law school, you know. They did give me some training.'

'In the law?' asked Nanny Piggins. 'Or did they just focus on training you to be the world's most boring misery guts?'

'They trained me to be a tax lawyer,' said Mr Green proudly.

'Same thing,' muttered Nanny Piggins.

'All rise for the honourable Justice Birchmore,' called Henry.

'If she does put me away,' Nanny Piggins whispered furtively to the children, 'and your father tries to feed you healthy food, remember, I have hidden chocolate behind the wallpaper in my room.'

'Which part of the walls?' asked Michael.

'All the walls,' said Nanny Piggins. 'There is an inch-thick layer of chocolate underneath all four of them.'

'How on earth did you do that?' asked Samantha.

'You can import chocolate wall-panelling from Switzerland,' explained Nanny Piggins. 'That's how they get through all those long cold winters in the Alps and why Swiss people are always yodelling so happily.'

Judge Birchmore made her entrance, striding to her chair.

'Be seated,' called Henry.

'Ah, Piggins, we meet again,' said Judge Birchmore gleefully. 'It seems you have been very busy in the interim. Busy flouting authority and breaking the terms of your probation, by the look of it.'

'She's also helped a lot of people!' yelled out Michael.

Judge Birchmore peered over her reading glasses at him. 'Don't think the fact that you are an unusually short child will stop me from sending you to a juvenile detention centre for contempt of court,' she warned, before turning on Nanny Piggins. 'Now, I have read the report from your probation officer.'

'I'm sorry,' mouthed the probation officer from the far side of the courtroom. (He was terribly upset. Much like the Retired Army Colonel he had fallen deeply in love with Nanny Piggins and her chocolate chip biscuits. He did not want to lose either one from his life.)

'He says he has sent you out to 17 different organisations, and you haven't lasted more than three days at any of them,' said Judge Birchmore.

'It's not my fault if it only takes three days to either solve all their problems or point out all their deficiencies,' said Nanny Piggins.

'And that you have bitten three community service providers, slapped another two and poked one repeatedly in the bottom with a nail on a stick,' accused Judge Birchmore.

'Ah yes, the litter collection supervisor. In my defence, it was a very large bottom,' said Nanny Piggins, 'and really, if your bottom is that big and you spend your whole day dealing with petty criminals with pointy sticks, you shouldn't be surprised if they are unable to resist the urge to poke it to see if it will burst.'

'Does your lawyer have anything to say in your defence?' asked Judge Birchmore.

'Send her to prison and throw away the key!' yelled Mr Green.

'I beg your pardon,' said Judge Birchmore. Even she, who had done so much to break the will and crack the spirits of the most seasoned defence attorneys, had never before seen defence counsel capitulate so quickly.

'Your Honour can't be seen to go soft on crime,' urged Mr Green. 'You can't let pigs like this run wild.'

Nanny Piggins turned on Mr Green. 'You're fired! You're even worse than Montgomery St John. At least he had the decency to pretend he had chapped lips and leave.'

'You can fire me,' said Mr Green picking up his briefcase, 'but I'm not leaving. I want to be here to see you get sent away for a very long time.'

'I like the cut of your jib, Mr Green,' said Judge Birchmore. 'I wish there were more lawyers like you. It would certainly make the trials much shorter.'

'See you in twenty years, Piggins,' said Mr Green, and he climbed one row back so he could watch the proceedings from the gallery.

'It now gives me great pleasure to announce my sentence,' said Judge Birchmore. 'You, Nanny Piggins, are a blight on society –'

'All she did was tightrope walk across to a slice of cake!' protested Derrick.

'And dent a few paperbacks!' added Samantha.

'Surely that's not a crime!' pleaded Michael.

'It's a crime if I say it's a crime!' screamed Judge Birchmore. 'And I say that you three are in contempt of court. Bailiff, once I give my judgement I want you to throw them all in the holding cells.'

'But your Honour, they're children! You can't –' protested Henry.

'Right, that's it!' screamed Judge Birchmore. 'When this trial is over I want you to throw yourself in a cell too.'

'Yes, your Honour,' said Henry, deciding a nice rest in the cells was just what he needed after an afternoon in court with Judge Birchmore. Plus it would also get him out of having to take his wife dancing.

'Sarah Matahari Lorelai Piggins,' continued Judge Birchmore, raising her gavel ready to pound the desk when she pronounced her sentence. 'For your blatant rule-breaking and crimes against decency, I sentence you to –'

'Stoooooopppp!' yelled Boris as he burst in through the back of the courtroom.

'What is the meaning of this?' demanded Judge Birchmore. 'Give me one good reason why I shouldn't lock you in the cells for contempt of court too.'

'Because if you do,' said Boris, 'I shall have no alternative but to take this matter to a higher court, where your original judgement shall be overturned and you shall be humiliated in front of the entire legal profession.'

This made Judge Birchmore pause.

'I have evidence,' continued Boris, 'that proves you should never have presided over Nanny Piggins' original hearing. You were unfit to do so.'

'How dare you!' hissed Judge Birchmore. 'What evidence?'

'Your former fiancé!' declared Boris, stepping aside to reveal the Retired Army Colonel who lived around the corner.

Everyone in the courtroom gasped – partly from surprise and partly from being really impressed, because the colonel was wearing his full dress uniform. (Being a military man, he knew how to look dashing.)

'You had a fiancé?' marvelled Henry the bailiff, emboldened by the fact that he was already headed for the cells and there was not much more that Judge Birchmore could do to him.

'Hello Letitia,' said the Retired Army Colonel, looking a little embarrassed as he waved to Judge Birchmore.

'Cyril,' murmured Judge Birchmore, a blush coming to her cheeks.

'His name is Cyril?' marvelled Nanny Piggins. 'I always thought his first name was "Retired".'

'Do you deny, Judge Birchmore,' said Boris,

striding to the front of the courtroom, 'that this man is, in fact, the love of your life?'

Everyone gasped again. The court stenographer actually fainted. She had worked in Judge Birchmore's courtroom for eight years and had no reason to believe that the judge was capable of any human feeling, let alone love.

'I've never seen him before in my life,' spluttered Judge Birchmore.

'Need I remind you, your Honour, that the punishment for perjury is imprisonment!' declared Boris.

'All right, all right,' said Judge Birchmore. 'We were *fond* of one another.'

'You were in love,' accused Boris.

'I held him in regard,' quibbled Judge Birchmore.

'You were in love. L-O-V-E love! And you cannot deny it, because I have proof!' declared Boris, holding aloft several sheets of pink stationery. 'The poems you wrote to the Colonel in which you describe, graphically and in rhyming couplets, your true feelings for him. Shall I read from them?'

'No!' screamed Judge Birchmore.

'Yes!' called Nanny Piggins. 'Please do.' She did not normally care for poetry. But in this instance she could not help but be curious.

Boris began reading: 'Oh how I love you, Cyril, like a nut is to a squirrel, like a flower is to a bee, is what you are to me –'

'I admit it! I was in love. I was in love,' yelled Judge Birchmore.

'Head over heels, giggly as a schoolgirl, squishy as a marshmallow love?' asked Boris.

'Yes, yes,' confessed Judge Birchmore. 'That sort of love.'

'Then I call upon my witness, Colonel Cyril Bryce-Chalmers, to describe the events of the evening of November nineteenth, ten years ago,' said Boris.

The Retired Army Colonel slid into the witness box, and Judge Birchmore straightened her wig, trying to make herself look more attractive.

'Letitia and I were sitting in my convertible being affectionate, you know . . . kissing,' began the Retired Army Colonel.

There were retching noises from the gallery as several members of the public tried and failed to not be sick.

'We do not need the graphic details,' said Boris. 'Some of us intend to eat later.'

'Some of us are eating now,' said Nanny Piggins, as she chomped on a nougat.

'We were sitting there when we heard this noise,'

continued the Retired Army Colonel. 'It was faint at first. But then it grew louder.'

'What sort of noise?' asked Boris.

'It sounded like a pig yelling "Wheeeeeeeeeeee",' said the Retired Army Colonel.

'Then what happened?' asked Boris.

'Well, the sound got louder and louder, until SMASH, a pig landed in the car right between us,' explained the Retired Army Colonel.

'And who was this pig?' asked Boris, triumphantly turning to the gallery.

'The defendant,' said the Retired Army Colonel longingly. 'The most beautiful pig in the entire world.'

'That's enough of this fiasco!' snapped Judge Birchmore.

'Oh no, it isn't,' said Boris. 'We are just getting to the nub of it, as your Honour knows full well.' He turned back to the witness. 'Colonel, describe your feelings for the defendant, Sarah Matahari Lorelai Piggins, who landed between you and your fiancée all those years ago.'

'It was love at first sight,' said the Retired Army Colonel as he gazed at Nanny Piggins. (Nanny Piggins sighed. She knew she should not be angry with men for constantly falling in love with her, but it did grow wearisome.) 'You should have seen her in the moonlight in her skin-tight yellow flying suit. She took her helmet off and shook out her chestnut brown hair, then turned to me and said – I'll never forget the words – "Sorry to drop in on you like that. Here, would you like a slice of cake?"'

'That does sound like me,' agreed Nanny Piggins.

'And the cake!' gushed the Retired Army Colonel. 'Yes, it was squashed from her landing but it was the most heavenly slice of vanilla whipped cream cake I've ever tasted.'

'And how did this affect your relationship with Judge Birchmore?' asked Boris.

'It was over,' said the Retired Army Colonel. 'I thought I was in love with her but once I saw Nanny Piggins I knew the true meaning of the word "love".'

'Can we stop this now? I think I'm going to be sick,' said Judge Birchmore.

'Me too,' agreed Nanny Piggins. 'Although that may be the six dozen lardy cakes I ate for breakfast.'

'It is all immaterial anyway,' said Judge Birchmore. 'I am a professional judge, I would never let my personal feelings affect my judgements.'

'Excuse me, your Honour,' interrupted Henry the bailiff, 'but that just isn't true. You let your feelings affect your judgements all the time.'

'Name one example,' challenged Judge Birchmore.

'Every time they serve fish in the courtroom canteen,' said Henry, 'you always get so incensed that you convict everyone on trial that afternoon and give them twice the usual sentence.'

'Well, fish is disgusting!' yelled Judge Birchmore. 'Whatever sauce you put on it, it still tastes like fish.'

'I can see why the Colonel prefers me to her,' Nanny Piggins whispered to the children. 'I think she's got anger management issues.'

Boris confronted the judge. 'You should have excused yourself from Nanny Piggins' trial as soon as you realised she was the woman who stole the love of your life,' he accused.

'You can't prove anything!' protested Judge Birchmore. 'I deny it all!'

'But you didn't, did you? You saw it as an opportunity for revenge, and you ruthlessly gave her a sentence 50 times greater than the sentencing guidelines!' Boris continued ruthlessly. 'Don't try to deny it – it's the real truth, isn't it?'

Judge Birchmore cracked, bursting into tears. 'All right, all right, I admit I did it. I wanted to punish the pig for ruining my life.'

She went on to say a lot more but it was hard to understand what it was, because of all the sobbing and sniffing and blowing her nose that followed. (People who do not cry very often tend to overcompensate once they get started.)

'Don't worry,' said Boris kindly as he patted the judge's hand (because he was, at heart, a very lovely bear). 'If you need a lawyer when Nanny Piggins sues you for wrongful community servicing, I'll represent you. I'm sure I can get you off if we plead insanity.'

'Hear, hear,' agreed Nanny Piggins. 'You only have to look at her to see she desperately needs a slice of cake and a good lie down.'

'Who is that bear?' asked Mr Green, leaning forward to his children. 'Where did he come from?'

'Um . . .' said Derrick.

'The firm should hire him,' said Mr Green. 'He is a brilliant trial lawyer.'

And so it was Judge Birchmore who was led weeping from the court, while Nanny Piggins was set free. Her community service requirement had been reduced to the much more reasonable 200 hours, which was easily covered by the work she had already completed, so they all went home to celebrate by eating lots of cake.

'Thank you, Boris,' said Nanny Piggins as she handed her brother another generous slice of honey cake. 'I'm so lucky to have such a wonderful and talented brother.'

'It was my pleasure,' blushed Boris as he burst into tears again. (He had been crying tears of joy all afternoon.)

'How did you get to be so good at being a lawyer when you've only had half a semester at law school?' asked Michael.

'I think I've just got the knack for it,' explained Boris. 'Being a trial lawyer is a lot like doing ballet. When you do ballet you glide about while everyone watches you pretend to be a swan. And in the law you glide about while everyone watches you pretend to know what you're talking about. It's the same skill set really.'

'You are certainly much better than Montgomery St John,' said Nanny Piggins.

'Yes, I know,' agreed Boris. 'That's because I made sure I had plenty of chapstick in my briefcase.'

'And Nanny Piggins, you will promise to stay out of legal trouble from now on, won't you?' pleaded Samantha.

'I will try,' promised Nanny Piggins.

'Really?' asked Michael.

'Oh yes,' said Nanny Piggins. 'I know going to jail sounds like fun. Being locked up with all those interesting people should be like one big slumber party. But I don't think I would like it because I would miss you three terribly.'

The children hugged her.

'So I promise to be good,' said Nanny Piggins.

The children sighed with relief.

'At least until Thursday,' added Nanny Piggins.

'What happens on Thursday?' asked Samantha, beginning to worry again.

'Isabella Dunkhurst gets back from Botswana, so I figure I can relax a little bit then,' explained Nanny Piggins.

The children hugged their nanny even tighter. They just had to accept that when your nanny is the World's Most Glamorous Flying Pig, the chances of her being in trouble with the law are always going to be slightly higher than for normal people.

ABOUT THE AUTHOR

R. A. Spratt is an award-winning comedy writer with fourteen years' experience in the television industry. She lives in Sydney with her husband and two daughters. Unlike Nanny Piggins, she has never willingly been blasted out of a cannon.

To find more, visit www.raspratt.com

If you're hungry for more Nanny Piggins
adventures

Nanny Piggins
and the
Daring Rescue

by R. A. Spratt

will be in all pig-approved bookshops
in September 2012